"Quiet, confident," she said, her tone more amused than flattering. "I like your style, Diego Santerra."

She drew him in far too easily. He wasn't there to make friends. Or anything else, for that matter. He was there to save her life.

"Just respect a woman who knows good salsa when she tastes it."

"Well, you might try some habañero peppers next time," she said, naming one of the spiciest peppers grown. "Perk it up a bit."

"You got'em, I'll use 'em. But I take no responsibility for your customers' stomachs."

She smiled. "Oh, we like things hot around here."

Diego looked up at her again, but there wasn't so much as a hint of innuendo in her expression or in her voice. No, that wasn't her style.

"Well, I'll see what I can do about that."

She paused a moment before answering. "You do that."

WHAT ARE *LOVESWEPT* ROMANCES?

They are stories of true romance and touching emotion. We believe those two very important ingredients are constants in our highly sensual and very believable stories in the LOVESWEPT *line. Our goal is to give you, the reader, stories of consistently high quality that may sometimes make you laugh, sometimes make you cry, but are always fresh and creative and contain many delightful surprises within their pages.*

Most romance fans read an enormous number of books. Those they truly love, they keep. Others may be traded with friends and soon forgotten. We hope that each LOVESWEPT *romance will be a treasure—a "keeper." We will always try to publish*

LOVE STORIES YOU'LL NEVER FORGET
BY AUTHORS YOU'LL ALWAYS REMEMBER

The Editors

SANTERRA'S SIN

DONNA KAUFFMAN

BANTAM BOOKS

NEW YORK · TORONTO · LONDON · SYDNEY · AUCKLAND

SANTERRA'S SIN

A Bantam Book / November 1996

ISBN 0-553-44538-3

Published simultaneously in the United States and Canada

Bantam Books are published by Bantam Books, a division of Bantam Doubleday Dell Publishing Group, Inc. Its trademark, consisting of the words "Bantam Books" and the portrayal of a rooster, is Registered in U.S. Patent and Trademark Office and in other countries. Marca Registrada. Bantam Books, 1540 Broadway, New York, New York 10036.

PRINTED IN THE UNITED STATES OF AMERICA

OPM 0 9 8 7 6 5 4 3 2 1

For Mark
This one is all yours.
The quest begins. . . .

Dear Reader,

Superheroes. At some point in our lives at least one of these "men with something extra" has sparked a fantasy . . . or two or three. But I've always had one favorite. So when my editor called to ask if I'd be interested in creating a superhero of my own, I chose my inspiration faster than you could slide a sword out of its scabbard. I wanted Zorro.

In fact, I have always wanted Zorro. He had it all. Dashing good looks, a commanding presence, and a strong sense of right and wrong. This notorious avenger willingly and repeatedly laid his life on the line in the name of honor and justice—without ever taking credit for it. But best of all, to me anyway, he did all this without any superpowers. He relied solely on his physical prowess and his wits. Well, okay. His body, his wits, and a really big sword.

Ah, a man after my own heart.

I thoroughly enjoyed creating my own superhero. Like Zorro, Diego Santerra is not your typical do-gooder. He's a reformed bad guy who doesn't consider himself all that heroic. He also relies solely on his skills and wit in seeking justice. Well, okay, so maybe he has a sharp blade or two tucked away in there also. And he goes to great lengths to avoid revealing his true identity.

There is one problem. You see, he thinks the life he repeatedly puts on the line isn't worth a whole lot.

I hope you enjoy your ride into the blazing hot desert. Diego Santerra will steal your breath . . . and brand your heart.

Donna Kauffman

ONE

Diego Santerra made a killer salsa.

He also made a pretty damn good killer.

This was the first time he could recall getting paid to do both.

He pulled the dusty green Jeep around the side of the small stucco building and parked next to the shiny black Harley Fat Boy he knew belonged to the cantina's owner. Blue Delgado.

He knew everything about Blue a person could learn from constant observation. The briefing he'd received in Miami three weeks before heading here to New Mexico had filled in the rest. Yes, he knew more about Blue Delgado than the Villa Roja residents who'd known her all her life.

Except for one thing. When would Jacounda strike? That was why he had agreed to abandon his anonymous surveillance and step inside the dimly lit little bar in search of a job. As a cook, of all things.

Donna Kauffman

2

Diego hadn't counted on the job being the one, and probably only, thing he did for himself, for whatever little pleasure there was in it. But he'd kept silent, agreed to the cover. He made it a rule to give away only what was absolutely necessary. And he had damn little to start with. So cook he would. Along with anything else that became necessary to get the job done.

It was that unshakable personal code that had made him first choice for Seve "Del" Delgado's elite tactical squad, known since shortly after its formation as Delgado's Dirty Dozen.

No one had to remind Diego that, almost ten years later, less than half the original team remained alive. And if Diego didn't complete this mission successfully, the next to fall would be Del himself.

He pulled his black Resistol down over his forehead a bit farther and pushed open the door to the bar. Even though it was barely ten o'clock in the morning, there were two men occupying barstools, sipping beer. Three more were playing pool on one of the two worn tables wedged into the space between the door and the bar. Several small vinyl-covered tables lined the wall by the front window, but they were empty.

Diego glanced once at the men, then dismissed them. He strode over to the end of the bar, propped his foot on the rail, and pressed his hands on the teak surface.

The bartender was an older Latino gentleman. Diego knew him to be Blue's uncle, Tejo Delgado.

The older man continued to wipe down a glass with the corner of his apron as he moved toward Diego.

"*Cervesa*, señor?" he asked, his accent noticeable, but not overwhelming. "Coffee?"

Diego shook his head. "I'm here about the job." He nodded to the hand-lettered sign taped to the front window. It had been put up only two hours earlier. "You need a cook."

Of course, the old man didn't have to know that Diego had known about the job opening yesterday. Del, or more likely another member of the Dirty Dozen, had seen to that little detail.

"*Sí*, that is true," Tejo said, "Señor . . . ?"

"Santerra." Diego straightened and offered his hand. "Diego."

Tejo smiled, revealing one gold-plated incisor amid a host of gleaming white teeth. "Ah, *Don* Diego. Just like in *Zorro*."

It wasn't the first time he'd been reminded of his fictional namesake, and would likely not be the last. He hated being back in the Southwest. "Something like that, yes," he muttered.

If the old man was aware he hadn't exactly flattered Diego with the comparison, he didn't show it. "Tejo Delgado." He extended his hand. "My niece Blue, she's the one you need to see, *amigo*."

Diego gave his hand a brief shake. He knew the man to be in his late sixties, a good ten years Del's senior, but there was plenty of steel in his grip. Diego wasn't surprised. Just as he wasn't surprised by the intensity of the quick yet thorough once-over Tejo gave him before releasing his hand. Diego expected nothing less from Del's brother.

"She have an office?" Diego knew the layout of the cantina as well, if not better, than the owners did, but he waited patiently for Tejo to answer.

He nodded to the side. "Past the end of the bar, third door to the left."

Diego nodded and pushed away from the bar.

"Knock first," the old man added.

Diego paused at the sudden edge in the otherwise friendly tone. He respected that. He also knew that there were few women on earth who needed that protective instinct less than Blue Delgado.

Until now, anyway.

He looked over his shoulder, dipped his chin once, then headed to the back of the building.

The door to the small office was old, scarred, warped from the heat . . . and standing open at least a foot. The room beyond was one large mass of clutter, in which the desk in the center seemed to serve as nothing more than an oversized paperweight. Keeping his word, he rapped the door once with his knuckles.

The woman seated behind the desk, nose buried in a stack of what looked like old-fashioned record books, didn't so much as flinch. He wasn't surprised. As far as he could tell, nothing fazed Blue Delgado.

"Enter at your own risk," she said, not looking up.

He'd heard her voice before, but only from a distance. Up close, there was a texture he hadn't heard before. One that slid across his nerve endings like a taut bowstring. Not only was it warm and deep, but there was a rough quality, as if she'd used it once too many times the night before.

He stepped inside and found a relatively empty space of floor near the front of her desk. Not in the least unnerved by her continued silence, he took the opportunity to run a once-over of the room in the daylight. The room was a bonfire of paper begging for a match.

And the potential for that to "accidentally" happen—preferably with an unaware Blue inside at the time—didn't escape him.

"In a moment." She flipped one book closed and shoved it aside to get to another one.

The hairs on his arms lifted in pleasure. He allowed himself the luxury of the sensation. It was all he'd likely get out of this job, and he wasn't a man to ignore life's small pleasures. His life didn't offer up any other kind.

Watching Blue Delgado for the past three weeks had not been a hardship. She was an incredibly striking woman. And she knew it. Diego respected that too. He never understood why anyone wasted time pretending to ignore the obvious.

Not that she flaunted the sleek waterfall of black hair that flowed down her back, or did anything to emphasize the prominent cheekbones and dark eyes handed down to her from her Spanish ancestors. She was of average height, but the rest of her body was a masterpiece of design. The clothes she chose were functional, not flattering, though he had to admit she could wear burlap and twine and still turn heads. Certainly his.

No, Blue Delgado's awareness of her fortunate genetics wasn't obvious. He knew by the way she moved. The way she spoke. Laughed. The way she rode that Harley of hers as if it had been built to be put between her legs for her exclusive use and pleasure.

She slapped the book shut and looked up. "What do you want?" The question was straight and to the point. Blue Delgado in a thumbnail description.

"The job as your cook."

She looked him over. The examination was swift and thorough in a way that would be the envy of some officers he'd had the displeasure of being interrogated by in past years. He didn't mind it in the least this time.

He was tempted to ask what his appearance had to do with his cooking ability, just to hear her answer. But he knew her sharp observation had little to do with the label on his jeans and everything to do with assessing the man that filled them. Something else he respected.

"You cook?" she asked.

"Daily."

She didn't smile, but the gleam that entered her black eyes was reward enough. "For more than one person at a time?"

"When I'm lucky." She was as sharp as she was beautiful.

Oh, this woman would be fun to play with. He'd known that after less than twenty-four hours on the job. He just hadn't expected to find that tantalizing bit of knowledge so difficult to ignore.

But then he hadn't expected he'd have to deal with her personally. Much less work for her.

None of which changed the bottom line. He'd broken more rules than he'd ever followed, but one he kept sacred was the division between work and play. Playing on the job got people dead.

She stood. He sighed inwardly. A damn shame, though. A real damn shame.

"The kitchen is through that door." She motioned across the hall behind him. "Lunch is in an hour. If you're still here by six and no one has threatened to shoot me." She paused to run her gaze over him again. It was totally impersonal and all the more erotic for the easy nonchalance. "Or you," she added, "then you have the job."

Diego held her gaze for just a split second beyond what was acceptable. At the door he looked back over his shoulder. "No ID or tax information?"

Her attention was already back on the open ledger in front of her. "If you're still here at six, I'll worry about it then."

"You don't even know my name."

She glanced up and nailed him with a steady look that made him glad he was on her side.

"You made it past Tejo," was all she said, then looked down again. She flipped open another accounting book, shutting him out more completely, more effectively than anyone he'd ever encountered.

Except perhaps her father. Diego's boss.

The man she and Tejo thought had died thirteen years ago.

Diego wrapped the apron strings around his waist twice and tied them in front, leaving the fabric a bit loose around his hips. His new uniform made concealing a gun impossible. Which was why Diego had learned long ago to arm himself in other ways. Actually, that instinct was inbred. He couldn't remember a time in his life when he hadn't spent each second fully cognizant of any and all potential threats.

Unfortunately, long sleeves were also out, so he had to find another place to conceal his knife.

He pulled a handful of datil peppers onto the chopping board and picked up the knife lying next to it. He'd been surprised and pleased to find the plump orange peppers in her stock. They weren't all that common. Sweet, hot, and just a shade too spicy for most people.

His thoughts turned to Blue. Yes, a shade too spicy for most people.

And Diego didn't believe in mild anything. Not salsa. And most certainly not women.

But Blue was off-limits. Giving in to a brief but heartfelt expletive, he turned his mind back to his work. Balancing the long kitchen knife on his palm, he tested the weight, then ran the edge of the blade along his arm. Every hair still in place.

He let out a disgusted sigh. "First thing we do is get your knives sharpened, Ms. Delgado." He quickly located the steel and set about honing every blade he could find, until each one could shave a man without benefit of warm water or shaving cream. At least the ones worth sharpening, which were too few, but enough to get the job done. The rest he tossed in a tray and shoved on a shelf over the stove within easy reach.

Never know when an extra knife or two might come in handy. And not just for cooking.

He made short work of the peppers, then quickly set about chopping the remaining ingredients to his salsa. His mouth curved slightly as he scraped the jalapeños into the mix. His salsa and plenty of chips would keep Tejo busy serving up *cervesa* while he started the quesadillas.

He had flour tortillas on the griddle and his mind on Blue Delgado's voice when the woman herself pushed through the kitchen door.

"Finding everything okay?"

He didn't look up from his place in front of the old grill. "You need new knives." He turned to the counter and began swiftly chopping onions. For a moment the only sound in the room was the sizzle of the grill and the rapid tap of his blade on the cutting board. Finished, he balanced the knife in one palm and reached for the chicken thawing on the counter.

"You don't seem to be having a problem with them."

His fingers tightened instinctively around the base of the knife, feeling the weight, the uneven balance. Not designed for throwing, he thought, automatically calculating the adjustments he'd have to make. As a means of distracting himself, it was a dismal failure.

"I sharpened the ones I could. You need a new steel too." He slowly relaxed his grip, but not his control. He was the cook. That was all.

At least that was what she had to believe.

A fact he was rapidly realizing he couldn't forget either.

He felt her move closer, knew she was scanning his work in progress. The muscles across his shoulders tightened. It had nothing to do with worrying about job performance.

He knew he could cook.

Just as he knew he could do the job he was sent here to do.

She stepped closer to him, then plucked a chip from one of the bowls he had lined up, ready to go out. He continued working on the meat, but watched with interest when she scooped up a healthy amount of salsa and slid it between her lips.

He began a mental count, waiting for the peppers to hit.

She merely smiled over at him. "Good salsa. If the rest is as good as this, you're hired."

She walked over to the industrial-size refrigerator and his chopping stilled as he found himself unwittingly caught up in the easy glide of her body. He welcomed the chill that swept briefly across the room as she pulled out a frosty bottle, taking her time popping the top.

"Bring the forms back with you at six," was all he said.

She helped herself to a slow pull, then another healthy shot of salsa. Popping the rest of the chip in her mouth, she caught and held his gaze, the beer dangling as if forgotten from her fingers.

"Quiet, confident," she said, her tone more amused than flattering. "I like your style, Diego Santerra."

She drew him in far too easily. He wasn't there to make friends. Or anything else, for that matter. He was there to save her life.

"Just respect a woman who knows good salsa when she tastes it."

"Well, you might try some habañero peppers next time," she said, naming one of the spiciest peppers grown. "Perk it up a bit."

"You got'em, I'll use 'em. But I take no responsibility for your customers' stomachs."

She smiled. "Oh, we like things hot around here."

Diego looked up at her again, but there wasn't so much as a hint of innuendo in her expression or in her voice. No, that wasn't her style.

"Well, I'll see what I can do about that."

She paused a moment before answering. "You do that."

Just then there was a loud commotion followed by the sound of at least two men yelling and glass shattering.

Despite the noise, Diego heard Blue mutter a rather earthy expletive. He turned back to his chopping, hiding the sudden urge to smile. "Sounds like you're needed up front."

Another round of shattering glass erupted, followed by a solid thud and the splintering sound of furniture breaking.

"Please, keep working. I can handle it," Blue said.

"Hey, I'm just the cook." Diego snagged her gaze as she turned to go. "Of course if it's the salsa they're fighting over, you just give a yell and I'll see what I can do."

She studied him for a moment, as if unsure what to make of her new almost employee. Diego let her look her fill, but inwardly cursed his newly fast tongue.

Stay quiet, stay in the background, observe, learn, protect. That was his function. He didn't like having to be reminded of that. Especially when he was the one having to do the reminding.

The bar fight didn't overly concern him. The only person he needed to worry about was standing in front of him. And from the sounds penetrating the thin walls, Diego doubted the altercation was anything other than a typical barroom brawl.

Finally she shrugged and let a hint of a smile curve her lips. On a soft sigh that got all tangled up somewhere inside him, she said, "A woman's work is never done."

Turning back to his chicken, he chopped a bit faster.

The uproar blasted louder for a second as the door swung open then muted slightly as it shut. Diego waited ten seconds, scraped the sliced chicken onto the cold half of the griddle, covered it, then moved easily and quietly to the door.

Not that anyone would have noticed if he'd knocked down half the pots and pans in the place. He eased the door open just in time to hear the cocking of a shotgun.

Blue's smoky voice somehow managed to rise above the din. "Flaco, take your hands off Jimmy and put the glass down before I blow away the only thing keeping your wife from leaving you. Tigger, I see you sneaking out the door. Since you suddenly seem in an all-fired hurry to leave after busting up half my place, why don't you do me a favor and send Sheriff Gerraro?"

"Blue, no, it's okay. No sheriff, *por favor.*"

The pleading voice belonged to Flaco. Apparently he was more afraid of the law than of disappointing his wife. Not a very smart man.

Diego shifted a bit so he could watch Blue. She nodded to the man at the door. "Okay, no sheriff. Tigger, you stay and help clean up this mess. You boys owe me a couple of new stools and a tray of mugs."

When Jimmy and Tigger opened their mouths to protest, she leveled a steely-eyed glare at them. "I'll forget the beer you wasted on my floor and the green felt I have to repair on the pool table."

To give them some credit, they held up under her intimidating stare far longer than Diego would have guessed. At least ten seconds elapsed before they finally nodded and silently went about picking up the remains of their fight.

Once he was certain everything was back to normal, he headed to the kitchen.

He was halfway to the griddle when he paused. Something wasn't right. He stilled completely and replayed the scene he'd just observed, focusing on the background noises.

When he hit on what had stopped him, he moved swiftly back to the hall. The door to Blue's office was closed. It had been open several inches when he'd stepped out minutes before.

Diego flattened his back to the wall and slid his hand to the black titanium knife handle that rode above the waistband of his jeans, just behind the edge of his apron. The knife slide free without a whisper. At five inches it was more than lethal. He balanced it in his fingers with practiced ease.

No light in the office. No noise.

Slowly, silently, he let the door drift on its uneven hinges, his back once again flat to the wall.

No reaction.

Diego crouched and moved closer behind the door. Just as he edged in enough to see inside there was a soft whoosh. Papers, a whole stack of them, cascaded to the floor.

He'd already memorized the layout of her office. His diving tuck and roll put him squarely behind the short end of her desk. More papers and folders went careening across the floor as Diego came up just over the edge of the desk, knife arm poised for immediate action.

Nothing.

The thud of a book snapped his attention to the window behind her desk. The darting shadow had barely registered when the knife was already winging in deadly pursuit.

It impaled the object in the upper left shoulder. Enough to slow and allow capture without causing unconsciousness. Perfect hit.

Unfortunately, he'd just nailed a poncho on a coat tree. He'd known it before the knife hit.

"Damn." He didn't usually make such an obvious mistake. That nine out of ten men would have not only fired, but "killed" this particular target did little to ease his frustration. He was better than that. He didn't make mistakes.

The falling book had simply tilted over the coat-rack. No one else was in the cramped room. But someone had been. Someone who had upset the precarious balance of chaos. Who? And had they been taking something . . . or leaving something?

Diego knew the caliber of men he was up against. Trained killers. He understood the mentality intimately. The only difference between him and them was motivation for the job they performed.

They wanted Blue Delgado as a bargaining chip to use against her father. And they would go about securing that chip by any means available. And when they were done, the chip would be expendable.

Diego's job was to see that they never had the chip

at all. He would also use any means available to him. His only edge was that he knew they were coming. They didn't know he was there. And if everything went down as planned, Blue would never know there had been a threat in the first place.

After all, it would be a little difficult explaining to her that she was being used as a pawn against a dead man.

A shout echoed down the hall from the bar, preventing further investigation.

"Oh, hold on to your backside, Gordo. Or better yet hold on to Joe's, he might enjoy that."

Blue's good-natured chuckle was drowned out by the raucous complaints of her customers.

"Yes, the food is coming," she continued. "Get the rest of that glass off the pool table, *por favor.*"

Her father had been right about one thing. The lady could handle herself. She was bold, confident, and as self-contained as any man he'd ever met. In a word, she was deadly.

To his instincts. And therefore to herself.

No time to deal with that now. It was enough that he'd learned his lesson early and with no real consequences. It wouldn't happen again.

He gauged the distance to his knife, still buried in the poncho. Too far.

Damn. And it was one of his favorites, though it served him right for being so damn trigger-happy all of a sudden.

He slipped across the hall and back into the

kitchen, taking his place at the griddle just as Blue came into the room.

"Fajitas almost ready?"

She'd just had her bar nearly trashed and faced down enough beer-fueled testosterone to put any man on edge, yet her voice flowed into his system as smooth and easy as the apricot brandy he knew Tejo kept stashed behind the flour canisters.

Diego shook his head. She was doing it again.

"Coming right up." He felt her pause hang in the air behind him like a breath trapped in his lungs. He also felt her gaze roam his body. It was as distinct and visceral as if she'd used two hands instead of her black eyes.

"Good."

One word shouldn't cause that deep, undeniable twitch low inside him. If he could just find a way of completing this job without having to listen to her voice.

She stepped to his side, leaning in to see what he was cooking.

He managed not to tighten every muscle in his body.

"Smells great." She put her hand on his biceps. It flexed hard, the instant reaction totally beyond his control.

She stepped away and he tried not to release an audible sigh.

"I'm taking this tray," she added, obviously referring to the one loaded with bowls of chips and pots of salsa. "Bring more."

So she thought she could command him as easily as a couple of drunks? "*Sí*, señorita. Pronto."

"See that you do."

There hadn't been the least trace of sarcasm in his voice, yet he knew she'd heard it loud and clear anyway.

The lady was sharp.

The lady was also going to be the death of them both.

There was a pause, then she said, "I'll have your paperwork ready to fill out just as soon as the afterwork crowd settles down. I'll give you your schedule before you leave tonight."

The job. He had to get back in her office before she did. "Fine," he answered, but a glance over his shoulder told him she'd already gone.

Diego arranged the bowls of fajita fixings on a large serving tray.

"Three more weeks, Santerra," he muttered. Three more weeks and Del would testify against Hermes Jacounda. And then, for all intents and purposes, Seve "Del" Delgado would cease to exist.

Diego would never see his team leader again. Or Del's daughter either.

No matter how badly he might want to.

TWO

Blue stepped into her dark office. She closed the door and leaned back on it, blowing out a long slow breath. Her new employee put a whole different slant on the word *intensity*.

For a man of few actions and even fewer words, he was the most controlled person she'd ever run across. Except, perhaps, for herself.

She'd watched him. Had found herself surprisingly unwilling to stop, in fact. His every movement and word was precise, nothing wasted. Direct with an answer, confident in his abilities . . .

And heaven knew he made a damn fine salsa.

The perfect cook. Certainly better than Leroy, whose cooking skills were marginal at best. He had lasted a whole six months before suddenly deciding to head east for greener pastures.

So why was she standing there debating how to tell her perfect cook that she wasn't hiring him?

She shook her head and pushed away from the door. She should just hire the man. Tejo liked him, after all. She smacked the light switch on just as someone rapped on the door.

She opened it and found her dilemma standing two inches away.

"Tejo needs you out in the bar."

She ignored the warm hum of his voice. "I didn't hear him buzz me."

"He didn't buzz. He shouted."

She'd been so lost in her thoughts, she hadn't heard him. She didn't offer up that information. "Thanks." She stepped past him. "You about done with the cleanup?"

"Close. Five minutes."

"Fine. Let me go see what Tejo's yelling about." She heard her uncle now, grumbling somewhat loudly in Spanish. "Meet me in my office in ten and we'll go over the terms of your employment."

"Will do, boss," her new cook said, then turned back to the kitchen.

So much for gratitude, Blue thought as she headed toward the front. Not that he'd looked smug. He hadn't looked . . . anything. Just a man who knew he could do the job.

She shook off the disquiet niggling at her instincts. Instincts she rarely defied.

The last time she had it cost her her home, her car, and five years of her life.

"Where have you been?" Tejo demanded, stomping toward her, wiping down a glass as if he had a personal vendetta against the water droplets clinging to it.

Her mind snapped out of the past, and with that came a measure of relief. And control. Blessed control.

She planted her hands on her hips. "I was about to give our new employee a rundown of Blue's rules before you so kindly bellowed."

Tejo paused in his wiping. "So you decided?" He didn't wait for an answer, but gave a sharp nod. "Good girl."

"Since when?" She smiled and shook her head. "Smart woman," she corrected. "Or trying to be for a change." Before Tejo could break into his favorite topic—that being Blue's life and what she should be doing with it—she went on. "You about ready to shut down for the night?"

"I am." He jerked his head to the window, frowning at her. "But Flaco out there has the idea that he can stay here in the bar tonight."

Looking past Tejo's shoulder, Blue could easily see the shadow of Flaco's old Ford parked next to her bike.

She turned back to her uncle. "He's not drunk. But Sandy heard about the fight and won't let him back in the house." Seeing the argument coming, she added, "He already gave me forty dollars toward replacing the glasses he broke, Tejo." She looked at the now covered pool tables. "He can toss a sleeping bag on one of them. He'll be fine."

"I don't care about Flaco's comfort. That's not my

worry and you know it. I don't like the idea of you being upstairs while—"

"I can take care of myself, Tejo," she broke in, trying hard not to sound defensive. "You of all people—"

"Problem?"

Both Blue and Tejo turned to find Diego standing in the doorway leading in from the back hallway.

Tejo started to speak, but Blue waved him silent. "Under control," she said smoothly. "You done back there?"

He nodded.

Without looking back at Tejo, she walked toward Diego. "Come on, then. Let's get this done so we can all go to bed."

If she hadn't turned her head at that precise moment, she'd have missed the brief spark that lit his eyes. Eyes so pale a blue it was as if the desert sun had bleached all the life out of them. It was barely a flash.

Her mind rejected it almost immediately. Her body was a bit slower on the uptake.

Was that the reason she was leery of hiring him? Because she might actually be attracted to the man? She could handle that. Handle him. She moved faster down the hall. "I have some rules. No big deal, but I do expect you to follow them."

"I'll be here on time. Everyone that wants to be fed will get fed. If I'm working during a mealtime, that will include me. I'll clean up before I leave. If that works for you, then you have a new cook."

Blue stepped into her office and waded behind her

desk before responding. He made it sound as though he was doing her a favor.

Actually, she supposed he was. She hated to cook. And her customers weren't too happy about her filling in for Leroy either.

Sifting through one of the many stacks on her desk, she swore for the thousandth time that she was going to clean out the whole place.

"Here, read this and fill these out," she said, handing him the folder and searching for a pen. When had the clutter exploded? She really had to get more organized, she thought with a frown. Now she was starting to sound like her ex-husband.

God forbid.

"I'll bring them back tomorrow." Diego folded the papers and slid them in his back pocket.

There was no denying the man had presence. After her divorce she had chosen to live out on the edge of nowhere, but the desert hadn't parched all of the feeling out of her body.

Santerra was tall, his shoulders a bit on the broad side, and his hips undeniably lean. In fact he was lean all over, but not in a slender, sleek way. No, he was more rangy. Raw. Her eyes flickered briefly to the sharp angles of his cheek and jaw. Hungry.

She blinked and looked back to her desk, spying a pen tucked between piles of folders. She slid the ballpoint out and reached across the desk with it.

"I have one, thanks."

She absolutely didn't blush. Not ever. The fact

that she came even close brought her head up and her shoulders straight.

"Fine." She dropped it back on the desk without a glance. "No drinking while you are on the job, not even one cold *cervesa*. Shoes are a must. Jeans and a T are fine, wear a clean apron every day. Follow all the health and safety codes listed on the sheet I gave you. If I get fined by the state because you break a rule, it comes out of your pay. I take care of the lunch crowd, so your day will start at three. Just leave me plenty of salsa. If things are slow, you get a dinner break, if not, you eat on the fly with me and Tejo. I won't expect you to cover anyone else's job. We close right about now every night. If the crowd thins early you can be out of here by midnight, except on Fridays and Saturdays. You have Sunday and alternate Mondays off. The hours are long, the pay isn't great, and your only backup for the time being is me. Start one fight and you are out of here." She paused for a breath, then said, "If that works for you, then you have a job."

His gaze never wavered, those bleak eyes of his unnerving. "I'll be here tomorrow at ten of three."

"No overtime pay." She smiled. "No brownie points either."

He patted his pocket. "The extra time is in case you have any other questions. No pay expected."

He glanced unexpectedly at her mouth, then back to her eyes. "No brownie points either." His voice was warm and rich.

She fought the urge to wet her bottom lip.

The sound of the bar door opening and shutting, followed by men's voices, filtered down the hallway.

"What's up?" Diego nodded casually to the doorway.

The tension in the room didn't lessen, but the focus shifted. Blue had the unmistakable impression that there was nothing casual in the request. Why? Was Diego afraid of something? Running from something?

Smart questions a smart woman should have already asked.

Like he's just going to tell you?

Still, she decided then and there that this employment was on a trial basis until he'd proven himself or until her instincts died down. Or until he proved her instincts right. Whichever came first.

The voices grew louder. Diego looked to the door then back at her. His expression was only mildly curious.

She still didn't buy it. She shrugged. "One of our customers is bunking here for the night."

"Drunk?"

"Homeless." She smiled. "At least until his wife forgives him."

"A regular, then."

"Regular enough." She ran a quick survey of her office. She really did need to come down a little early in the morning. So much for the target practice she'd planned.

She moved out from behind the desk. "See you tomorrow, then."

Diego shifted to let her pass. He purposely did not look across the room where his knife was still twisted into the poncho. He'd come back immediately after she'd headed up front to talk to Tejo, but had thought it wiser to listen in to their conversation.

And now good ol' Flaco was going to put a damper on his planned after-hours unguided tour.

At least the increased mess in her office hadn't raised any unwanted concern. If all went as planned, Blue would never know she was under his protection. Or that her life was in jeopardy.

Or that her father was the cause of it.

"Diego?"

He turned at the sound of her voice. Which sounded way too good speaking his name. "Right behind you."

He pulled the door shut behind him, tugging a bit to make the warped wood settle tightly in the frame. "You don't lock up?"

She kept moving down the hallway and she shook her head. "Nothing in there to steal, really. Not that they could find it if there were."

He didn't ask where they kept the day's receipts or petty cash. She wouldn't give that information to a new employee. And he already knew the answers anyway. "Business so good you don't have time for office work? Maybe you should hire someone."

She stepped behind the bar; Diego crossed in front of it.

"Office work doesn't get done because I hate it.

And the only new employee I can afford is you. Unless of course you want to moonlight."

"No thanks. I'm just a cook."

She looked him over with obvious speculation. "And a damn good one too."

Her praise hit a string that had been out of tune so long he had to stifle his heartfelt response. "It's a living."

Tejo and Flaco's voices echoed from the basement storeroom. Diego took in the bedroll on top of one of the pool tables, then scanned the rest of the room quickly before turning back to Blue.

She was staring at him again and didn't make any effort to stop when he caught her. He said nothing, just stared in return. Never make the first move unless you have no choice.

"You've done it for a long time, then?" she asked.

"You asking for references?"

She shook her head. "Your cooking is your reference. And as long as you follow the rules, you'll have a job here."

In other words, she didn't trust him—not yet, anyway—but was fair enough to give anyone a decent chance. Diego didn't want to think about what would have happened if one of Jacounda's men had discovered that particular streak of hers and taken advantage of it.

She'd be living on borrowed time. And Del would be dead.

Because Diego knew if it came to it, his boss would sacrifice the trial and his life for that of his daughter. He already had thirteen years earlier for his wife, Blue's mother. Only that time he'd lost. Lost it all. His wife had died and his only child had lost her father for a second time. Only this time she truly believed him dead. There had been no other way to keep her safe.

But safety was an illusion. So was security.

Del had divorced her mother when Blue was barely seven. But his wife had eventually been caught in the deadly web of her ex-husband's career anyway. This time Del had officially died the same night his wife had. Tejo and his wife took over the job of keeping Blue safe. And they had.

Until Hermes Jacounda managed to discover Del's true identity.

It was only a matter of time before Jacounda found the one bargaining chip he had in the trial that would almost certainly put him in prison for life. Blue.

"I can live with your rules." He had to get back in here tonight and find out what—or who—had happened to Blue's office earlier. And get his knife.

"Why is it I get the impression that you only abide by rules if they suit you?"

He gave her his full attention. "Because you are a smart woman."

"Are you in any trouble I should know about?"

"No."

"Quick answer. Would you tell me if you were?"

"I wouldn't involve anyone else in my business."

"Interesting answer."

"I'm just a cook."

She smiled. "Yeah, right."

For some reason he had a hard time not smiling back. "See you tomorrow."

An hour later Diego pulled the Jeep behind the pueblo that was at the center of the small town of Villa Roja. Blue's Place was about a hundred and fifty yards down the main road, the last building before the highway disappeared into the desert. There were no buildings behind the cantina either, but the rocky terrain leading out to a crumbling mesa provided cover for any one of a number of predators.

Diego shook his head. It was way too vulnerable. He'd set up surveillance of her place shortly after his arrival, but it hadn't been easy. Del had originally put two men on the job, but they had decided early on that the town was simply too small to absorb the presence of two men without drawing attention. Fellow teammate John McShane was still close by in Taos if Diego needed assistance.

He slid noiselessly from the truck and just as silently crossed behind the row of buildings fronting the main drag. He moved farther back toward the mesa when he neared Blue's. The second-story light illuminated her bedroom window. Having her live over the bar did help matters considerably.

The quarter moon provided an equal amount of light and shadow. Diego made good use of both. He'd managed to scope out the immediate area behind the cantina when he took out the trash while closing up.

There were footprints in the dirt lot. Too many, in fact. But none directly under Blue's office window. Which meant the intruder had either been clever enough to remove that evidence or they had come in through the front door.

And it was the possibility of the latter that had caused Del to send Diego inside.

Intelligence back in Miami had no direct proof that anyone in Jacounda's organization had headed west. But they were also smart enough to know that he or someone who worked for him could have hired outside talent for this job.

Diego found his gaze drawn back to Blue's window. Complex woman, Blue Delgado. What in the hell was she doing out on the edge of nowhere? He knew about her marriage and subsequent divorce. Much of that had been documented. It had been rough on her. Her husband had been a fraud, a user. He'd talked her out of the police academy and into a higher-paying job, then over the next five years while she climbed the corporate ladder, he'd proceeded to bilk her out of almost everything she owned.

She didn't strike him as the type of woman who'd allow something like that to happen to her. She struck him as a survivor. Much like her father. Would a philandering liar of a husband really be enough to send a woman like her into seclusion?

Diego didn't know the answer to that. Love did strange things to people. He had no experience in that kind of relationship. Not even close. And given that stories like Blue's seemed all too frequent, he intended to keep it that way.

He stood perfectly still, watching her window, keeping his senses on full alert. He stood just like that until at last, some ten minutes later, the light went out.

He let out a long sigh he'd had no idea was inside him.

Yes, his life was exactly how he wanted it.

He carefully picked his way to the back door, not disturbing so much as a stone to mark his path. He was inside in less than sixty seconds. He swore under his breath, hating both Blue's lack of security and the threat that would rob her of that naive trust.

He moved cautiously toward the front. Flaco was snoring soundly on top of the pool table. He'd observed Tejo leave for his home and wife shortly after his own departure. That left Blue. He listened closely but heard no movement overhead.

The sudden urge to climb the backstairs and check for himself that she was safely asleep in her own bed was surprisingly strong. And alarming. The urge had nothing to do with her safety. He knew she was up there. Alone.

He turned away from the stairs, resolutely shutting out the images of Blue lying in her bed, and slipped into her office. Using a tiny beam of light, he edged his way to the coatrack. Seconds later, his knife safely tucked by his side, he moved cautiously back to the desk. Pulling one of Del's little toys out of his jacket pocket, he quickly ran a scan over the room. No electronic devices. Detonating or otherwise.

He lifted the phone, dismantled it with ease, flashed his beam of light inside both the receiver and the base unit. Clean.

Diego's initial impression seemed to be correct. Whoever had been in there had been looking for something, not leaving something. What, though? Proof they had the right woman? No, Jacounda's men were too thorough. There were too many ways to check that out without running a careless B&E during business hours.

That last little part had been bugging him too. He was given no time to analyze the puzzle. A whisper of noise from the kitchen caught his full attention.

He moved as swiftly as he dared in that direction, stopping, back flat to the wall, just outside the swinging kitchen door.

There it was again. A soft whoosh. The freezer door, he deduced as he edged closer. He could still hear Flaco softly snoring, which narrowed the identity of the early-morning raider to two. Blue. Or an intruder. The soft groan of pleasure he heard in the next instant narrowed that field down to one.

He ignored the tiny race of pleasure that shot down his spine at the throaty sound, even as he found himself placing his fingertips on the edge of the door, intent on a quick verification that Blue was indulging in a night treat. But another sound, a low rustling followed by a muffled thump, sent him retreating swiftly down the hallway to the rear exit. He eased the door open in time to see a black shadow stooped by the window of Blue's office. Moving silently, hands loose and ready, he'd almost closed the distance when the intruder suddenly stood and swung around.

"What the—"

Diego lunged, but the other man, smaller and wiry, darted unexpectedly to the side. He dashed off into the moonlit desert. Diego knew better than to give chase and possibly lose him in the desert. The knife was out and perfectly balanced in his hand in a natural motion. He centered his weight, pivoted, and took a bead on the running man. The knife was winging through the night air bare seconds later.

A high-pitched scream ripped into the silence, followed by a loud grunt and thud as his target tripped and fell to the ground. Diego had closed half the distance to the fallen man when the back door slammed open. Damn, Blue had heard the scream.

Diego barely had time to take a dive around the side of the building when the bright light of a halogen lamp lit up the entire rear area of the cantina.

That was immediately followed by the sound of a shotgun being cocked.

"Who's out here?"

Diego swore under his breath. Stupid question, Blue. Not like you. If he hadn't been certain the intruder was out of action with a knife in his lower left shoulder, he'd have taken her down in a flying tackle. As it was, he stayed in the shadows.

"Blue?" The word was more croak than shout. "That you?"

Diego's attention jerked back to the wounded intruder. There was movement and moaning, but it wasn't threatening. He looked back to Blue. She took a half step forward, then stepped back again. Smarter. She kept the gun steady and shoulder level, her eye never leaving the site.

"Answer me!" she shouted. "Who's there?"

"It's me, Le—" He broke off on a cough and a long moan "Leroy," he eventually rasped out, the sound barely carrying over the quiet desert night.

"Leroy?" Blue walked toward the fallen man, but kept the gun up.

Diego's respect for her bumped up a small notch.

"What the hell are you doing out here?" she asked, concern for her former employee's health not in evidence. Give him hell, Blue. He was glad to see her generous streak didn't extend to being gracious to ex-employees breaking and entering.

Of course Diego had no business smiling. This was a development he certainly didn't need. Leroy was supposed to be working in the Florida Keys right now. His unexpected return was not a good sign.

"I came . . . back," Leroy choked out. "Could you . . . call 911."

"Oh, I think that can be arranged. In fact, it's been done."

Diego nodded his approval even as he swore under his breath. This he definitely didn't need. The decision to leave before the local law showed up was balanced against his absolute need to know why Leroy had traveled all the way across the country to break into his former boss's cantina.

If he could just get his knife back. His prints were on it. Of course, he doubted Leroy would leave it alone, and so the risk of his own prints being found was minimal. But he'd just gotten it back.

This was not turning out to be his day. He was just thankful John wasn't there. He was probably the only human being alive who felt comfortable enough in Diego's presence to give him a hard time. Of course the fact that John was a walking lethal weapon did tend to balance the scales a bit.

Blue closed the remaining distance, then angled the barrel of the gun directly at the head of the still-downed Leroy.

"Tell me what's going on before Gerraro gets here, Leroy. What were you doing out here snooping around my place at two in the morning, and how did you get hurt?"

"I didn't want anyone to see me talking to you." He groaned again. His voice was thin and whiny. "I'm bleeding, Blue. I need help."

Her voice gentled a bit. "It's on the way, Leroy. Where are you bleeding?"

She lowered the gun, but not out of range of usefulness. Diego wondered at her natural ease with the firearm. The logical assumption was that Del had taught her, but he'd been gone since she was a small girl. His reappearance in her life thirteen years ago had been tragically brief. And she hadn't been in the academy long enough for extensive training.

Had Tejo taught her?

"My shoulder," Leroy answered. "A knife."

Blue lowered the gun the rest of the way and knelt by Leroy's side. "My God, Leroy. You were in a knife fight?"

"Uh . . . not exactly."

Diego watched as Blue checked out Leroy's shoulder. "For heaven's sake, Leroy, this isn't just some little switchblade here. What in the hell happened?" She didn't let him answer. "I can't take it out. I'm afraid it would make you bleed worse. It's in the fleshy part of your shoulder, though, and it's not bleeding too badly. I think you'll be okay. The rescue squad should be here any minute."

Leroy's head fell back to the ground. "Good. It really hurts, Blue."

Diego couldn't see her face, but he could hear the mix of disgust and amusement in her tone. "Yeah, I imagine it does. Why don't you take your mind off of it while we wait and tell me what you're doing back here. I thought you were in Florida."

"I was. Great job."

"So why come back? Surely not because you missed working for me," she said dryly.

"It was too good, Blue. I got . . . curious." His voice faded, making it hard for Diego to hear, but he didn't dare try to move closer. As it was, he'd have to split as soon as the first squad car arrived. The sirens in the distance told him that was about thirty seconds away.

Hurry, he willed Leroy.

"I found out something. I had to warn you."

"Warn me? Leroy, what in the world could you find out in Florida that has anything to do with me?"

"I think someone is trying to kill you, Blue."

"Don't be ridiculous."

"Well, I was going to call—" He broke off when the sirens grew closer. "But I wasn't too sure they wouldn't have you bugged."

"I think you've lost more blood than I thought. You're delirious."

"No!" He shook his head, then groaned. Cars pulled into the front of the cantina with a loud squeal of sirens and flashing lights.

Diego strained to hear Leroy's next words.

"Someone is trying to kill you. And I was right. Because tonight they tried to kill me."

THREE

Diego barely bit off the harsh epithet. What in hell had happened? Someone had gotten dangerously careless. And now one skinny cook with a conscience was going to blow this whole thing to hell and back.

They had to get Leroy out of there before he was questioned. Gerraro was not your typical small-town sheriff. Diego had been briefed on him before arriving. Vince Gerraro had been a homicide cop in Detroit for fifteen years before heading south for warmer, less violent climes. Del had toyed with the idea of bringing him into the case, but anyone not on the team could be made vulnerable too easily. The one distinguishing factor of the remaining Dirty Dozen members was that not one of them had a single attachment outside the team. No family, personal or extended. Invulnerable. Inside and out. Anything less rendered the team ineffective. The work they did was highly sensitive. And high risk.

Diego moved to the front of the building as the two occupants of the sheriff's car headed around back on the other side. He was in his Jeep and on a scrambled cellular line—another of Del's toys—in less than two minutes.

A gravelly voice answered on the first ring. "Yeah?"

"I need to get into my safe-deposit box."

"It can be opened for you." The voice was fractionally less rough and Diego knew he had John's full attention.

"I need help getting the stuff over there, though." He glanced down the street at the sheriff's car, which was now accompanied by an emergency rescue vehicle. "It's going to be wrapped in brown paper for a while and I need to get it out first."

"Need any Red Cross volunteers?"

"Nope. Already have two of them. Maybe I can get my stuff from them more easily. Worth a try."

"Sounds like a plan. Be there in ten or fifteen."

"That should be just about perfect."

There was a pause on the line. "I take it that would be a welcome change right about now."

"So true. Nothing gets done right with everyone talking all the time."

Diego heard the softly muttered curse. "I'll see what I can do about getting you some peace and quiet."

"Probably too late for that. It's amazing how fast news travels."

Another softly muttered curse. Diego understood

his frustration. Then John said, "Let's just hope people don't believe everything they hear."

"Rumors do get out of hand. I'll work on that here."

"See you in ten."

"I'll be there."

The pause was briefer this time. "The one thing I can count on, my friend." The line went dead.

Diego sat there for second or two longer, holding the phone. It wasn't all that unusual for John to make a statement like that. It was the flip side of all the grief he gave Diego. John was the team member Diego worked with most often. Their styles and personal combat techniques suited each other well. Though the whole team was close-knit, the bond was strictly professional. Even life-and-death bonds were held at arm's length. John pushed that barrier. Diego frowned. So what else was new?

But for some reason Diego couldn't pinpoint, this time it gave him more than a little pause. Made him feel . . . connected.

Dangerous thing. Even though he'd always been fully dedicated to the team's mission and would give his life for any one of them, they all remained doggedly independent. Of anyone, even—and to a degree, especially of—each other. Caring got you or your rescue target killed.

The ambulance drove out of Blue's lot, lights flashing but siren off, drawing him back to the moment. But the relief he felt in letting his mind settle into familiar strategy-developing patterns was somehow just as disturbing.

He knew the nearest hospital was in Taos; a twenty-minute drive. John was located there, his presence easily absorbed into the much larger population. They'd have Leroy out of the hospital—and Gerraro's hands—and in a safe house where they could question him, in under an hour.

He'd work on ferreting out Blue's reaction to Leroy's news tomorrow. He doubted she'd believe such an outrageous claim without proof, something he'd make sure she'd never get. So that ruled out her doing anything impulsive or dangerous tonight. He'd waited long enough to see the sheriff's car leave and watch her go back into the house. Leaving her alone was a calculated risk he'd have to take. That he didn't like it . . . and that his problem with it was only partially case-related had him pulling out of the lot with a bit more speed than was wise.

But then thinking about Blue tended to do that to him.

With a harsh curse he turned his attention back to more solvable problems. Like how he was going to get his knife back. Again.

Blue watched Gerraro and his deputy leave. The ambulance had taken Leroy to Taos and Blue knew that was where the sheriff was headed. She'd argued about heading in with them, but Vince had told her he'd call her in the morning. Blue debated briefly about following them anyway, but she finally went back into the cantina. She knew she should call Tejo. He'd undoubtedly hear about it long before he got in to work and should really hear it from her. But she was a bit more shaken up by Leroy's message than she'd let on to any of them and she needed time to sort it all out first.

In all the excitement, Flaco had decided to head home and try to get his wife, Sandy, to let him in. Blue knew Sandy's fuse was short on both ends and didn't think Flaco would be back. It also meant the grapevine would be humming by sunup.

She put her shotgun away and trudged upstairs. Even though she knew she wouldn't be going to sleep, she climbed between her blankets and sheets and settled her head on a stack of pillows.

Someone wanted to kill her.

Leroy's claims were ludicrous. And murder was simply too ridiculous to give any credence to. But he'd been so certain. . . . And while Leroy hadn't been the most dependable person in the world, he hadn't been a liar either.

But who would want to harm her? Much less kill her? Sure, there were people in town who thought that running a bar was a less than respectable thing for a woman to do. Especially when the woman in question was a divorcée. Though why that made a spit of difference she'd never been exactly sure. She was fully aware of the things some of the more small-minded said and the less than kind labels attached to her on occasion.

Her reaction had always been a mixture of amusement and disinterest.

But murder? No. No one had any personal ax to grind with her as far as she knew. Except maybe for Anthony. Her ex-husband certainly had no love lost for her, but that was only because she'd finally exposed him for the sweet-talking, two-timing, charm-you-while-he-robs-you-blind son-of-a-bitch he really was. Yet Anthony didn't have the guts to harm, much less kill anyone. He avoided trouble, rather than looked for it. He was far more likely to spend his energy on finding a new mark and reinventing himself all over again. Blue didn't waste any further thought on that possibility.

Vince Gerraro was good at his job and would find out where Leroy had gotten his information. No sense belaboring it further until she talked to him in the morning. She'd try to get in before opening the cantina to see Leroy, too, if he was still in the hospital.

Sleep finally drifted in to claim her. But one last thought before she dropped off ensured her sleep would not be peaceful.

No matter how strange and unlikely Leroy's claim . . . the fact remained that someone had knifed him. A very skilled someone.

"What do you mean he's gone?" Blue shouted into the phone. She didn't worry about keeping her voice down. The cantina wasn't open yet. Tejo was the only one up front. "How could you lose him?" She swore under her breath as the sheriff explained that Leroy had been admitted to the hospital and treated, but due to some complications he didn't fully comprehend, they'd sedated him. He'd waited at the hospital for several hours, but when he finally poked his head in Leroy's room, the bed was empty.

"I still don't understand how a sedated man with a knife wound could simply get up and walk out of the hospital." Another thought occurred to her. "Unless you think the person who knifed him came back and—" She broke off, forcing herself to calm down. "That's ludicrous. Isn't it?"

"I don't know what to think, Blue. I doubt anyone carried him off, but the EMT that transported him said that several times on the way in, Leroy claimed he was certain he was being followed. More than likely he was afraid, and when he came to and got up to go to the bathroom or something, he managed to get away without us catching him. The lounge was not in direct sight of his door."

"Vince—"

"Hey, it's not like I thought he was a flight risk. I don't know what happened behind your place, Blue, or where he got the idea you were in danger. For all we know he's the one in trouble. More likely story, if you ask me. But if you want, we can send someone by the cantina on a regular basis. It might be wise if you call me with a description if you see anyone frequenting the cantina or hanging around town."

"Do you really think that's necessary?"

"I've got a bulletin out on him. I have a few calls in

to the PD in Miami to see what we can dig up on him or in case he shows up back there."

That made Blue pause. "Do you really think there is anything to his story?"

"Did he have any drug history? There didn't seem to be any indication of that last night, but those test results aren't available yet."

"No, not that I ever noticed. He didn't seem high or anything last night either. He was in a lot of pain, but he was scared. And adamant . . ." she added, her voice trailing off.

"Blue, listen, can you come down here sometime today before the cantina opens and answer some questions?"

"Officially?"

Gerraro laughed, the sound slightly reassuring. "Listen, this is the most excitement I've had since leaving Detroit."

"I thought that was why you came here." She could almost hear his shrug and fought a smile. Vince was a good man and an even better cop. He'd hinted more than once that she'd make a good one herself. If he only knew . . . She shoved that thought away.

If Vince wanted her to come in and talk, she would. "I'll be there about ten. I need to be back by eleven to get ready for the lunch crowd."

He laughed again. "Hey, and don't think this won't be good for business. Word gets out, and you know it will, you're likely to have more customers than ever before."

"I'm thrilled," she deadpanned.

"You got that new cook now, you'll be all right."

Blue didn't bother asking how he'd heard about Diego when she'd hired the man less than twenty-four hours earlier. In a small town, your business was never completely your own.

"He's okay. You'll have to stop in and try his—"

"Salsa. Yeah, I heard. Hey, just a thought, but what do you know about this guy?"

A sliver of a chill ran down her spine, making her shudder lightly. This was exactly the question her subconscious had buried the night before. Now she had to face it.

"Not much." She wanted to ignore her clamoring instincts, but realized she no longer could.

"Just a word of caution, Blue. I know you are careful out there, but keep an eye and ear open. If you feel anything the least bit out of the ordinary about this guy, call me."

Blue didn't know whether to laugh or groan. Oh, the things Diego Santerra made her feel were anything but ordinary.

"In fact," he went on, "why don't you let me run a check on him for you."

"No," she answered instantly. "I mean, I can handle Santerra. If I think otherwise, I'll let you know." She didn't want to get into this. Not now. Not ever, if the truth be told. She just wanted a cook, she railed inwardly. Was that so much to ask?

"Okay. For now, Blue. But if I feel that it's called for—"

She cut him off. "Yes, fine. Listen, I got a million

things to do if you want me there in an hour." The phone had barely hit the receiver when the door to her office swung open after a light rapping.

She jumped in surprise and was immediately disgusted with herself. Lack of sleep, she told herself, not buying it for one second.

Diego came into the room and slid on one of the stacks of paper she'd been making since five in the morning.

"Sorry, watch where you step."

He stepped carefully to her desk. "And here I thought it couldn't get any messier."

She shot him a glare that would have other men stuttering and backing up in quick retreat while they still had all their body parts intact. Diego merely looked bored.

"Why are you here?"

"*Buenos días* to you too."

She huffed out a sigh of impatience. "Listen, I've had a rough night and I have less than hour to make most of this." She waved her arm to indicate the stacks of paper. "Go away."

Diego plucked a Blue's Place matchbook from the tottering heap on her desk and offered it to her. "Won't take five minutes, tops."

"Very funny." She fought a smile, though. His sense of humor was so dry you could choke on it. "And tempting," she admitted, and looked up at him. "So, why are you here so early?"

"Heard about the trouble you had last night. Thought you might want some help with the lunch crowd. Figured you'd be down at the sheriff's office pressing charges."

Blue made a sound of disgust. "I wish." She shook her head, not meaning to say anything more. "They lost Leroy. Can you believe that?"

"Leroy?"

"One of my old employees. He was my last cook." She paused, then added warily, "Just how much did you hear?" She'd told Tejo early this morning before he'd heard, so she hadn't gotten the grapevine version. "I'm surprised you're already plugged into Villa Roja's hotline. Outsiders usually have to wait at least a day to catch up."

"I didn't hear much. Just stopped in down the street for a couple of eggs and some coffee and overheard Flora talking to some of her regulars. Said someone tried to break in but got hurt."

"Stabbed."

"Why Señorita Delgado, I'm impressed. Handy with fire- and sidearms."

"I didn't stab him. They don't know who did."

"Did you find out what he was after?"

"Oh, he wasn't after anything, he was trying to—" She broke off. Why was she telling him this? The sheriff's warning to find out more about her new cook echoed in her mind. "Never mind. It's moot now that he's gone."

"You don't worry he'll come back?"

She shook her head. "I doubt that very much." In an abrupt change of subject, she said, "Did you fill out the forms?"

He pulled the folded papers from his back pocket and tossed them on her desk.

She smoothed them open, more relieved than she cared to admit that she finally had more concrete information on the man. But for some reason, seeing his bold script filling all the lines did little to quiet her still-grumbling instincts.

She scanned them quickly, noting he used a post office box for an address. She looked at him. "I'll need a physical address as well."

"I don't have one."

"Excuse me?"

"No street, no address."

"Where are you living? Out in the desert?"

"I have a trailer up in hills a bit, about ten minutes from here."

"It takes at least ten to get to the state route that leads back there."

"I just head straight back. My Jeep can handle it." The corner of his mouth curved when she lifted a brow. "Guess I never believed the lines on the road were my friends." He nodded toward the window and the parking lot beyond where her Harley was parked. "You always keep that hog on the highway?"

He had her there. She lifted her chin. "Most of the time."

"Yeah, right. So, you want me back at three, then?"

It took Blue a split second longer to switch gears. For a quiet man, he pulled her in easily. Too easily.

"Actually I do have to step out for a few. I'll be

back before the lunch crowd, but I could use some of your salsa."

"Sure." He turned back at the door. "If you need anything else, let me know."

She nodded, wanting him to leave so she could read his forms. But a flash caught her eye as he moved through the door. His light jacket lifted away from his body as he stepped over the last pile. A black clip hung on the outside of the waistband of his jeans. As if sensing her sudden attention, he looked back as he stepped into the hall. She quickly averted her gaze, and he left. But she had the unsettling feeling that he knew where she'd been looking. And at what.

The clip was tucked on the inside of his jeans. It looked like a holster or a sheath of some kind for a knife.

And it was empty.

Diego sealed another container of salsa, squeezed it in the now-packed refrigerator, then began to clean up. Blue had left shortly after their chat and, three hours later, had yet to return. He'd overheard her conversation and knew she was headed to the sheriff's office. He'd contacted John, who had followed him back from Taos after dropping off Leroy with two other team members, and knew she was being kept under close observation. He trusted John with his life—had, in fact, several times over.

So why was he pacing the kitchen like a cat on a hot rock?

Grumbling under his breath, he rinsed off the last of the knives, dried and stored them. He quickly wiped his hands on his apron, then yanked at the strings and all but tore it off.

Four out of the six Dirty Dozen team members had been called into this case now. There could be no more mistakes, no more unraveling threads, and most definitely no more loose lips.

Leroy was no longer a threat, but the information he'd given to Blue was still not entirely neutralized. John would find out what, if anything, she'd told the police. Diego's job was to find out if Blue believed Leroy's claim. He had to talk to her.

If she ever came back from the damn sheriff's department.

He balled up his apron and threw it. Tejo caught it against his chest as he came through the swinging doors.

"Problems, *amigo?*"

Diego quickly quelled his disgust at being caught in an entirely uncustomary display of emotion. "No," he answered. "Just done what I can do here for the time being." He reached out for the apron, but Tejo shook his head.

"I'll dump it in the basket for you."

"Thanks." Diego finished the last wipe-down of the counter then shot the rag at Tejo, who caught it with a quick flashing smile.

"You leaving until your shift this afternoon?" the older man asked.

Diego nodded. "Unless you or Blue need me here."

"We're fine. Blue should be back shortly for the lunch rush." His expression tightened a bit. "Looks like we'll be busy too." He paused, as if debating whether or not to speak further. Then, on a huff of frustration, his accent thickening, he said, "Damn town is full of rubberneckers. One hint of trouble and—" He snapped his fingers, then snorted in disgust.

"It's all over now." Diego walked over to the man. "Besides, it's just that many more people paying to drink your *cervesa*. Right, *amigo?*"

Tejo looked up at him and Diego had to fight the odd sense of déjà vu. Not that Del and his brother looked all that much alike. But every once in a while Tejo's expression would match one he'd seen too many times on Del's face. Worry.

"*Sí*, Don Diego," Tejo responded. "But there is something here that is not right."

"What? Have you had trouble like this before with Leroy? With anyone?"

He shook his head. "No, that is just it. And Leroy, well he's not the brightest boy, and Lord knew barely a cook, but he thought the world of Blue. If he thought she was in trouble—"

"He'd travel halfway across the country to warn her when he could have picked up the phone? Unlikely for a two-bit cook, don't you think?"

Tejo looked at Diego with probing black eyes. "You're just a two-bit cook. What would you do?"

Diego didn't take offense. He did, however, go on full alert. Tejo wasn't buying his "I'm just a cook" routine. Apparently gut instinct ran strong in the Delgado family. "Depends on the situation. It just seems Leroy could have found another way to contact Blue if warning her was his real motive."

"You have a theory, then?"

Diego shrugged. This was the sort of conversation he needed to have with Blue. Where the hell was she? "Drugs, money, trouble with the law. There are a dozen reasons someone with no funds would flee cross-country. But with technology what it is, I just don't buy the warning thing." He checked the switches on the griddle and stove, his demeanor making it clear the subject was only of marginal interest to him.

Turning back, he brushed his hands on his thighs. "Guess that does it here. Tell Blue there's plenty of salsa in the fridge and I set up some quesadillas that just need to hit the griddle for a few minutes. There's also some—"

Tejo laughed and held up his hand, his worries at least temporarily on the back burner. "Whoa, whoa. Blue's idea of doing lunch is an all-you-can-eat taco bar." His expression changed to one of tender amusement, but his tone was a bit wistful. "Cooking is not a skill she ever managed to pick up. Alethea, that's my wife, she used to do all but tie Blue to a stool to get her to learn to cook." He laughed again. "Not that child. She was an outdoor creature. Still is." His expression sobered as he glanced at the clock.

Diego felt the man's concern, as it echoed his own. Tejo's instincts were to be trusted, something Diego wouldn't forget. But John was watching Blue, and now was not the time to let Tejo get too worried.

"Blue spent a lot of time with you growing up, then?"

Tejo turned back to him. "Yes, her parents were killed at a young age. She's been part of our lives for a long time." He shook his head. "You know, she wanted to be a cop, took after her dad that way." His deep sigh spoke of pain and loss. "You should have seen her with my brother, Seve. Ah, but they were a pair. They had so little time together and yet you have never seen two human beings closer than my niece and her father. I'm not sure who idolized the other more. But the thought of her following Seve into law enforcement . . ." He looked away, then back again. "Alethea and I talked her out of it. We were selfish. We'd had too much death and sadness. She was all we had. We wanted her safe." He snorted. "Safe. She tries to do what she thinks is expected and ends up with that no-good—" He broke off, muttering under his breath. "After that she came out here, bought the cantina. I come in from Taos to help her out." He looked around. "I guess she is safe now." He shook his head. "But happy? I don't know. I guess you always think you should have done better."

"She's lucky to have you. Her childhood wasn't an easy one."

Tejo's shoulders squared a bit, his Spanish heritage clear in the broad lines. Pride filled out the rest. "Yes, she is. You remind her of that when you see her next. Since I plan to take a strip off of her if she isn't back in here shortly."

Diego knew his harsh words were simply a cover for his increasing concern.

Just then the wall phone by the door jangled. Tejo scooped it up. "Blue's." He listened for a second, then swore loudly and fluently in Spanish. "That was a damn foolish thing to do," he shouted into the phone, one hand gesturing as he spoke. "I've told you before not to take that death machine out there. If Alethea hears about—" He stopped abruptly.

Diego could hear Blue's heated voice through the phone from several feet away. On full alert, he still found himself fighting a smile. She might not have inherited her aunt's love for cooking, but she had inherited the Delgado temper.

"Carrying a cellular phone isn't good enough. You should be—" Tejo broke off again, listening for a few seconds. "Okay, *sí*, yes." He fell silent again, nodding occasionally.

"I'll be there shortly." He sighed, then sternly added, "Don't go anywhere. Stay put."

Diego heard her laughter as Tejo slammed the phone back on the receiver. "Problem, *amigo?*"

"Blue ran that machine of hers out into the desert and got a flat tire. That girl, I tell her again and again and it's like talking to a brick wall. I swear she—"

Diego cut him off, his concern tripling instantly. John wouldn't lose her. His tracking skills were legendary. But what in the hell was she doing traipsing all over the desert?

"Can I help you out? I can go get her. I'm done here."

Tejo's expression brightened. "Actually, that would be a good solution. Unless you are as good a bartender as you are a cook."

"Sorry. Beer and the occasional whiskey straight pretty much exhausts my knowledge."

"Fine, then, you go get her. Thank you." He turned and grabbed an order pad from the counter. "This is where she is." He started scribbling on the pad when the phone rang again. "So help me, Saint Joseph, if she's been bitten by a rattlesnake or something I'm going to kill her myself," he grumbled as he snatched the phone up. "Blue's."

Diego watched his eyebrows lift in surprise.

"Hold on, he's right here." He extended the receiver to Diego. "For you."

Diego took it, dread creeping down his spine. Only two people had this number. Only one would ever contact him on it.

"Hope you don't mind that I gave out this number."

Tejo shook his head. "As long as it doesn't interfere with your work."

Diego nodded. "Hello?"

John's voice came across the line. "Problem, *amigo.*"

"What?"

"Our mutual friend. I lost her."

FOUR

Blue peeled off her chambray shirt and twisted the white V-neck T-shirt she wore underneath into a knot above the waistband of her jeans. Lord but it was hot as hell.

Where was Tejo anyway? She sighed and raked her hair off her forehead. She'd hated calling him, having lost count of the number of times he'd lectured her on her impulsive desert jaunts on her Harley. Now, with a flat tire and a healthy serving of Tejo's crow stuck in her throat, she still didn't have her head on straight.

Two hours at the sheriff's office had done little to help. In fact, it had been those two hours that had sent her screaming off into the desert in a cloud of dust. She hated being confused. After her divorce she'd purposely reduced the number of complications in her life to the impersonal and banal to avoid that very thing. Now she had death threats to think about.

Was Leroy telling the truth? And if he was, was the only new face in town her potential attacker?

She really didn't want to think about that last one. A good cook was simply too hard to come by, she told herself. But her insouciance felt much more like bravado.

He was a cook with an empty knife sheath.

A cook she'd known two days who had already infiltrated far too much of her mind.

Diego Santerra a killer?

A killer who made good salsa?

The roaring of an engine jerked her mercifully off her mental merry-go-round.

She shadowed her eyes with her hand and watched the dust plume rising along the desert floor behind Tejo's truck.

Except it wasn't Tejo's truck.

It was a Jeep. A dark green Jeep. Diego's Jeep.

Blue hated the dread that crawled down her spine as she watched him approach.

She looked around her. For what, an escape route? She'd always sneered at the heroines in movies who stood wringing their hands, awaiting their fate. Until she'd become one of them.

She turned to her saddle-bags and rooted around, trying to find anything she could use as a weapon. "Wonderful," she said in disgust, holding up an elastic cord. "I'll just bungee him to death."

The truck came closer. She grabbed her keys and held them tightly in her fist, one pointed end protruding between her knuckles. It wasn't much, but it was about all she had.

Her gaze fell on her cellular phone. Duh. She should have called Gerraro immediately.

Heat rose off the ground, casting the Jeep in wavy shimmers as it cut across the baked land, less than five hundred yards away.

Too late now.

Besides which, he'd never have gotten to her in time.

Blue shivered even as the sheen on her skin turned to beads of sweat. But at least they'd know who'd taken her.

Unlike Leroy.

Diego pulled the Jeep up next to her bike and swung out the open side. Blue braced her legs shoulder width apart and centered her weight, trying to be prepared for any move he might make.

What really shook her was how she reacted, or how her body reacted, to the mere sight of him. She swore his legs went on forever. They were long, lean, with jeans that fit him perfectly. His dusty boots only added unneeded length. His white T stretched tightly over his shoulders and chest.

The sun was at his back, and she squinted up into his face, struck again by the unexpected sexy contrast of his dark hair and dark eyebrows and lashes with those impossibly pale blue eyes. Emotionless, yet mesmerizing.

Dangerously so.

He lifted his hand and she instantly dropped into a ready crouch.

"You okay?" His brow furrowed a bit as he held out a large bottle of springwater. "I know it's not a cold beer, but . . ."

A killer who offered water to his intended victim? Blue supposed there were far stranger occurrences out there. Still, her cheeks heated as she stood and accepted the water. He watched her silently as she uncapped the plastic bottle.

Some latent survival instinct kicked in as she pressed the edge to her lips. She pretended to drink but held her lips closed, then held out the bottle. "You want some?"

His eyes sparked with amusement. He hadn't missed her ploy at all.

Was he just toying with her before taking her out?

Taking her out? Oh Blue, you really do need to get in out of the heat.

Finally he shook his head. "No, help yourself."

Had she heard a challenge in his voice? She shrugged. "That's okay, I've had enough."

"I'm sure you have."

"Did you come all the way out here to give me a lift or harass me?"

"A little of both, it would appear. But I intended only to give you a ride."

"What about my bike?"

"We'll take the tire off and have it repaired or you can get a new one. I'll bring you back out later to put it on."

Blue's wariness persisted despite his casual tone and cool logic. "That's not necessary. I can just drive Tejo's truck out. I'll put in a call to a mechanic friend of mine who has a trailer. I can tow my bike. Besides, I need your services more as a cook than a grease monkey."

"You'll never get a trailer out here." She simply crossed her arms and stared at him. He lifted a shoulder in half a shrug. "Suit yourself." He squatted beside her bike, then looked back up at her.

She drew in a short, shallow breath. When the sun hit his face he looked wild and beautiful. His eyes were almost eerily seductive. Her skin prickled again, the sensation not at all unpleasant.

Sunstroke. She was suffering from sunstroke.

"You know how to take this thing off?" he asked.

"In fact, I do. You don't?" She really didn't want to smile.

He shrugged. "I'm—"

"I know, I know, just a cook." With everything else going on, she really didn't want to be charmed by him. "You don't need to bother anyway," she said. "I'll get the trailer."

"You don't intend to come back out here tonight, do you?" It was the first time she'd heard even a hint of emotion in his voice.

"I'm not leaving my bike out in the middle of nowhere all night."

"What do you think will happen to it way the hell out here?"

"I'm not leaving it here."

He held her gaze for another long moment, then stood and brushed his hands on his thighs. "Fine, then let's go."

For some reason his attitude rankled. Blue had been all prepared to argue with him, something, anything, whatever it took to get rid of all this tension she suddenly seemed to have wound up inside her. And he'd robbed her of that pleasure.

Ten minutes ago you thought he wanted to kill you. Now you're complaining because he's being too nice?

Killer or cook? Hell, she didn't know what she thought at this point. She just wanted to get out of here.

She walked around and slid into the passenger seat. He was already in and belted.

They bounced over the desert for almost ten minutes before the silence became almost as intolerable as the dust swirling inside the Jeep.

"Where are the doors to this thing?"

"Don't have any."

She looked at him. "No doors?"

He didn't glance at her. "Never needed any."

Blue stifled a sigh. "Where is Tejo?"

"The grapevine is in action. Your cantina is the hot spot today, it seems."

She swore under her breath. She may have reduced the clutter and responsibilities in her life to a bare minimum, but the ones she did have she took seriously. "He should have just left me out there to bake."

"He did mention something about that as I left."

"Very funny."

She thought she caught the edge of a smile in the corner of her vision but refused to give in to the urge to look at him. Again.

"He should have asked you to stay and take on the lunch group."

"I left him with plenty of salsa and quesadillas. They'll survive. Besides I don't think anyone will leave till you make an appearance."

"Lovely."

They rode in silence for several minutes. Then he said, "Do you come out here often?"

The personal question surprised her. The warmth his interest stirred disconcerted her. Blue stared out the windshield at the never-ending vista of golden-brown earth, dotted with the occasional sage and saguaro. The majestic buttes and mesas jutted suddenly upward, like some sort of violent life-forms erupting from beneath the sands, the earth no longer able to contain them. She identified with that feeling, that need to erupt, to break free.

She thought she'd done that when she'd divorced Anthony and relocated to Villa Roja. But had she?

No. The response was as instant as it was final. She'd just traded one guarded existence for another, safely contained once again just beneath the surface of an insulated, risk-free life.

And she had no idea how to burst through the surface.

Her heart tightened as she continued to scan the landscape before her, seeing her life there too. Endless. Dry. Dangerous only when you strayed from the established paths.

She wanted to stray. Oh yes, she did.

"Yeah, I come out here," she said quietly. "All the time."

"It can be beautiful, peaceful." His voice was quiet, soothing. Nonintrusive.

Yet she was vitally aware of his presence next to her.

"It is for me." She wanted to look at him. The very strength of the pull kept her from doing it. "But not for you," she added.

The pause that followed wrapped around her like a physical touch. It both seduced and unnerved her. She wanted him to keep talking, wanted to sustain this link she felt to him. Yet she felt the inherent danger in doing so. And it had nothing to do with fear for her life.

"What makes you say that?"

She shrugged but still avoided looking at him. If they spoke and didn't make any contact, even eye contact, then it was almost like talking in the dark. Another safety screen. Another illusion. She clung to it.

"You just seem on edge out here. Not uncomfortable, just . . ." She drifted off, feeling silly all of a sudden.

"I was raised out here."

She did look at him then. He was staring out through the windshield, his profile hard and impenetrable. She knew he saw more than the dusty tracks in front of them. What was he seeing? Remembering?

"If you don't like it, why not move away?"

"I have. Many times."

She returned her attention to the desert. "Yet you keep coming back. Maybe you should think about what draws you here. Figure it out, give in to it. Maybe then the pull wouldn't be so strong."

"I know what pulls me here."

The truck slowed and she felt him look at her. Her muscles tightened until they almost vibrated under the sensation. Her fingernails were digging into her palms before she even realized she'd made fists. She carefully relaxed them, and the rest of her body.

"At least this time I do."

Adrenaline shot through her, almost making her jump.

Her. He had as much as told her he'd come here for her.

What do you want? she wanted to shout. *Who in the hell are you?*

"I needed to get away from everything for a while," he went on, his attention back on driving, the truck resuming its normal spine-cracking speed. "This is the best place I've ever found to clear your head."

Blue blinked a few times, keeping her attention firmly on the tracks they were following. Had she just read too much into his words? Imagined that entire exchange?

"That's why I came out here today," she said.

"Did the sheriff's department find anything? Has Leroy turned up?"

She jerked slightly at the question. She shook her head. "No leads." Oh brilliant! Just tell him everything. Sorely distracted, her answer had been reflexive. The jarring ride must have knocked her common sense loose.

She glanced sideways at her rescuer. She liked to think she was sharp, alert, but suspicion was not a normal emotion for Blue. Her gaze slid down to his waist, where she knew an empty knife sheath was tucked out of sight on his other hip.

In the next instant she felt the heat of his return scrutiny. Knowing she should just let her attention move easily and quietly elsewhere didn't stop her from doing the last thing she should have.

She looked up.

The Jeep rolled to a stop just a few feet shy of the highway.

"Something wrong, Blue?"

There were too many responses to his casually asked question. And right now she felt anything but casual about all of them.

Are you a killer?

"Why did you come out here today?"

His brow furrowed a bit, her only clue that her question had not been the expected one. Which begged the question *What had he expected her to ask him?*

"That's fairly obvious."

"Saving the boss's butt is not in your job description."

She felt his attention on her sharpen.

"You didn't have to come out here," she went on. "Tejo could have gotten a number of people to do it. Especially if the cantina is as crowded as you say."

"I offered. He took me up on it."

"You should have stayed in the kitchen."

"You're welcome, no problem."

Blue's cheeks heated. She hadn't exactly been gracious.

But wasn't there something a bit weird about thanking the man who might be out to kill you? What etiquette rules applied in this sort of situation? *Gee, thank you, and oh, by the way, you weren't out here trying to kill me, were you?*

Then again, when the hell had she cared about etiquette? Or rules for that matter.

But Alethea's constant nagging apparently hadn't been a total waste of time. "I'm sorry. Thank you for driving out here. I do appreciate it. I'll put you on the clock for your time."

"It was a favor, Blue. No payback necessary." He didn't return his attention to the road. It was focused totally on her.

Formidable was the word that came to mind. Unusual for a cook.

But not for a killer.

"Suit yourself," she said finally. Her temples began to throb.

She heard him mouth something under his breath. *If only I could.*

But before she could think it through, he checked

his rearview mirror and pulled the Jeep onto the highway. Heading in the wrong direction.

Head pounding and adrenaline still zinging, she worked hard to keep calm. "The cantina is that way." She pointed to her right.

"I know."

There was a hard edge to his voice she'd never heard before.

Striving to stay cool, she said, "Well, if the cantina is as packed as you predicted, maybe we'd better head that way now."

He wasn't gunning it, but they weren't crawling along either.

"You need to get the trailer. I have a hitch."

His words were calm, completely casual. She glanced at his hands. They were relaxed on the wheel.

Then why did she get the feeling he was screaming with tension?

Mind tricks. Leroy's wild story had obviously taken deep root.

She glanced in her rearview mirror. There was a dark car behind them. But it was so far back, it was more a shimmering mirage in the heat emanating from the blacktop than any threat. Real or imagined.

"How do you know where the trailer is? I never told you." She studied him now, wondering if she should have challenged him.

"There is only one garage near Villa Roja and it's located on the way to Taos. I just assumed that's where it was."

A coincidence? Logical conclusion?

"Well, as it turns out, you are right. My friend the mechanic owns the garage. He's a biker too. We ride together sometimes. I'm sure he won't mind."

"Fine. We can hook the trailer up now. I can go back out later when things die down and pick it up for you."

"I told you, I'll take Tejo's truck."

"No sense in hooking it up twice. Besides, I imagine you'll get caught up in the local hoopla. I can go. No problem."

Blue should feel relieved. But she didn't. A glance in the rearview mirror showed the black car had closed the distance slightly.

Was it her continued out-of-control imagination, or was Diego checking his rear mirror a bit more often than habit called for?

"If it's dark, maybe we should wait till tomorrow."

"I thought you didn't want to leave it out there. I can get there between the afternoon and night shift."

She felt the Jeep increase in speed. The black sedan was still closing in on them.

"You might want to slow down, the garage is just ahead."

Diego nodded but kept his foot firmly on the gas. It was clear that Blue hadn't dismissed Leroy's warning. She'd also begun to wonder if the only new person in her life might be a threat to her safety. To her very life. But he couldn't worry about diminishing her suspicions at the moment.

When John had called to tell him that his tire had blown and he'd lost Blue on her hell ride into the desert, Diego had assured him he knew where she was and was on his way to get her. Then John dropped the real bomb. Word had come to him just moments before leaving on his wild chase that some Miami talent was on its way to audition for Hermes Jacounda in New Mexico.

Diego flashed another quick glance to the outside rearview mirror. Would any of Jacounda's boys be so blatant and obvious about their choice of transportation? A black sedan? Or was Hermes sending Del—and by association, Diego—a message? We're coming to get her and we don't care who knows it?

With Jacounda, it was likely the latter. And that meant life was about to get real interesting for Blue and her new cook.

Diego let his foot off the gas, but they were still going at a pretty fast clip as they came to the garage. At the last possible moment Diego pulled hard on the wheel and whipped the Jeep into the lot. He pulled to a stop away from the building and the two pumps, which were surprisingly modern considering the overall dilapidated appearance of the place.

Blue had one foot out the door before the dust settled.

The black sedan slowed down. Then flipped on its turn signal.

Polite talent, Diego thought.

He didn't glance at Blue, but felt her shift her weight, preparing to jump down.

"Stay here for a minute."

He saw her turn from the corner of his eye.

"What?"

The driver pulled the sedan into the garage slowly, as if this had been his destination the whole time. And maybe it had been. Which was why Diego had made sure to park as clear from both the pumps and the building as possible.

"I said stay in the Jeep for a minute." He hadn't taken his eyes off the sedan. She was looking at it now too.

"Friends of yours? Trouble catching up with you, perhaps?"

She sounded almost relieved at that possibility. He decided to let her be. It suited both of his purposes for the moment.

"Just stay here for a minute."

He took her long sigh as an agreement and slid out of the Jeep. No one had exited the sedan, which was pulled up to the diesel pump. The sedan wasn't a diesel.

Diego felt the empty sheath on his hip. John had managed to retrieve his knife from the sheriff's department, but he'd kept it for the time being. Carrying around a weapon that had been placed at a crime scene was not a good idea.

Diego put his hand on his belt buckle, casually releasing the lock guard on the knife it contained. It was much smaller than his usual weapon of choice, and not balanced for throwing. But it did give him another element of surprise in hand-to-hand combat.

The driver's door to the sedan opened as Diego stepped farther out into the open area between the pumps and the building. If there was a mechanic or attendant on duty, they hadn't shown their faces.

Wise choice.

A tall, very stocky man with no neck and perfectly cut pinstripes clambered out of the car. Diego whistled silently. A shame to mess up such a nice suit. If things went smoothly, he wouldn't have to.

The big man's face was wide, hard-angled, and otherwise nondescript. His eyes were hidden behind black Wayfarers. Diego didn't need to see them. The color may vary, but he'd seen the eyes of this man and a hundred other like him. They were all the same. Stone cold and empty.

Diego was very familiar with the look. It was the same one watching him shave every morning.

Diego walked easily, casually, to the pump island, staying behind the car. He reached for the window squeegee and snagged a few paper towels, keeping No Neck in his peripheral vision the entire time.

It was a calculated risk putting himself out in the open and leaving Blue unattended in the Jeep. But John was due in shortly with a tire needing repair.

Better to find out who they were dealing with now, when he was controlling the situation.

A smaller, skinny man was in the passenger side of the car. He had short, curly black hair and an acne-scarred face. Diego could almost feel the wired energy emanating from the little man. He also recognized him. Jimmy D. Freelance killer.

No one would look at the two men and pick

Jimmy out as the lethal one. Which was precisely why Jacounda had sent along No Neck.

Jimmy had been on Del's list for years. That Hermes had sent him to take Blue was also a message. A very smug message. It was also a mistake.

Diego slowed his movements, hyperaware of everything yet detached, almost as if observing the entire scene surrounding him from a seat in a theater. He missed nothing.

The instant the passenger door shifted the first fraction of an inch, Diego swung into action, drawing no undue attention to himself.

He came around the back of the car, as if heading back to the Jeep, and dropped his paper towels. They made no noise, but they caught No Neck's attention. Diego crouched down to pick them up, slid his knife from his belt and sliced it along the right rear tire all in one smooth movement. A quick glance showed that No Neck was coming around the car.

The sound of gravel crunching stopped the big man's progress. He swung around to watch a large four-by-four pickup truck lumber into the gas station lot.

Diego made his move. The passenger door swung open, blocking any view of what he was about to do from the Jeep. He had no idea if Blue was watching all this, but he was thankful that she wouldn't have to see it. Made his job much easier. No messy questions to answer. And there were far too many messy questions that could be asked in this case.

Jimmy swung his legs out, his right hand by his

thigh. Diego registered the nine-millimeter Glock he carried. Simultaneously bringing up his knife and a fistful of paper towels, he took out Jimmy's gun hand first. The wad of paper towels in the small man's mouth muffled his screams. A well-placed chop with the side of his hand took out his right knee. Jimmy wasn't going anywhere.

Diego shoved Jimmy back into the seat just as he heard John shout out a friendly request to No Neck for a hand with his flat tire.

What followed was more tightly choreographed than the most challenging of ballets. No Neck turned to respond to John as Diego flipped the seat latch, flattening out the seat and putting Jimmy on his back.

With his knife on Jimmy's jugular vein, Diego leaned into his face.

"Hey, Jimmy," he whispered. "Should have stayed in Florida. Didn't anyone tell you the desert can be murder this time of year?"

The smaller man never even blinked. A true professional stone-cold killer. Diego knew John would likely get nothing out of the man. But Jacounda would eventually know that he'd lost his first team. And sending that message would be enough this time around.

Fifteen seconds, a belt, and two bandannas later, Diego was certain Jimmy wasn't going anywhere. At least not until John escorted him there. He was also fairly certain the smaller man wouldn't bleed to death before John had his turn with him. But it was a calculated risk he simply had to take.

A loud thud told him that John had taken out No Neck. He didn't have to look to know that it had been done as unobtrusively as Jimmy's exit from the game had been. Diego almost smiled. He knew John had not only been up to the challenge, but had relished it. Unlike Diego, who did his job because he believed in it and did it well, John actually enjoyed his work. Craved it, in fact. Diego had never asked what demons drove John, just as his occasional partner had never pried into Diego's background.

But if he had to rely on anyone, it was John McShane.

Diego left the squeegee on the ground under the car and headed to the building. The sounds of air wrenches and metal tools clanged from inside the garage bay. He found the mechanic on his back under an old Ford pickup.

"Hey there." He shouted to be heard over the din. The sudden cessation of noise made his ears ring.

The grimy coveralls protruding from beneath the truck slid out to reveal a barrel-chested man with a full black beard and a long braid. "Hiya." He pulled a set of headphones out of his ears. "Hope you haven't been waiting long. What can I do for you?"

"Friend of yours needs to borrow your bike trailer."

The man's deep laugh echoed off the walls. "Blue's been playing in the desert again. She send you in here?" The man stood and wiped his hands on the towel hanging from his waist. He was head and shoulders taller than Diego. Still chuckling, he extended his hand. "William Maxwell. But everyone calls me Tiny."

Diego took his hand. "Pleased to meet you, Tiny."

"You must be the new cook."

"Yep."

Tiny walked over to a side door. "Follow me, it's out back." He opened the door and stepped outside. "I have to tell you, though, it's not like Blue to send anyone in to do her dirty work. Especially a man, if you know what I mean. Guess she's snowed under at the cantina. Meant to get over there myself today, but got sort of involved here."

Diego had to admit he was more than a little intrigued by Tiny's casual reference to Blue's apparent aversion to men. Had her ex soured her on men altogether?

Just as Diego opened his mouth to ask Tiny what he'd meant, he was saved from his lapse in judgment when Blue peeled around the corner of the garage in the Jeep.

She was out of the truck and storming down on him before he could close his mouth.

"What in the hell were you doing out there? That guy in the pickup just towed that car away. Towed that gorilla in the monkey suit away with it. You're over there doing goodness knows what and then you just stroll into the garage like nothing is happening? What is going on here?"

FIVE

She was right in his face. Diego couldn't remember the last time someone had invaded his personal space the way Blue did. He sure as hell knew he'd never enjoyed it before.

"I was going to get you to wash the dust off the windshield while I got the trailer. The guy in the car had a problem, but the other guy in the pickup said he'd help them out." Diego shrugged. "We need to get back to the cantina, so I came in here looking for your mechanic friend."

Diego was well aware that Tiny was watching this interchange with no small amount of interest. Whatever was said here was likely to be spread all over Villa Roja before sundown. He could use that to defuse suspicion. But for the moment he was having a hard time taking his eyes off of Blue.

"They were following us," she said. "I thought

you were in trouble, that they were after you or something."

"After me?" He gave Tiny a confused look, then turned back to Blue. "What gave you that idea? I'm just the—"

"Don't even say it." She swore under her breath. "So I'm paranoid now, is that it?"

Tiny broke in. "Well, Blue, what with Leroy saying someone's out to kill you and all." He patted her on the shoulder. "It's understandable you'd be a bit on edge, darlin'."

Diego actually had to bite back a smile. Up until now he'd thought Tiny was a smart man.

Blue spun around and bore down on the big man. "Don't use that tone with me, William Maxwell. I know what I saw, and those men were after Diego." She stopped abruptly, her mouth still open, then turned to face Diego. "Unless they were after me."

His chest tightened in an uncontrollable little clutch, followed closely by a keen sense of rage. He'd never thought to see vulnerability in Blue's eyes. He was suddenly mad, killing mad, at the man who had put it there.

"We came out of the desert. In my Jeep." He paused for a brief second, not entirely sure he had his voice totally under his command. The realization did little for his temper. Control had always just been his. Harnessed, fully contained, there for the asking.

Until now.

Until the need for it had become personal.

"No one could have known where we'd hit the

highway. How could they have been after you?" he said calmly. He'd never felt less calm. His heart was pounding so hard he was surprised she couldn't hear it, see it beating beneath his damp T-shirt.

She started to argue, but stopped again, staring out at the desert for several long seconds. Diego let her have her moment, his motives not entirely selfless. Tiny was smart this time and also stayed silent.

She turned back around and faced them both. "Okay, so maybe this whole thing is bothering me a little more than I thought it was. I just wish I'd had the chance to question Leroy again."

His respect for her grew as he watched her grapple for and gain control. She was an intelligent woman with good instincts that were telling her she was not making this up. It didn't seem right for him to take that away from her.

But her sharp instincts would do her no good dead.

"I'm sure he'll turn up somewhere. He seems a bit unstable if you ask me."

"He never was before."

"He up and took off for Florida with no notice," Diego argued.

"See, that's what's bugging me. That was just not like Leroy."

"Well, he did it. Obviously he had things going on in his life you knew nothing about. You have no idea what he might have been involved in."

He watched her struggle to accept his logic. His admiration grew again. Instinct pitted against relentless cold logic rarely survived. Blue's was still alive and kicking. She'd have made a good agent. As good as her dad. And that was the highest compliment Diego could bestow. He respected few men. Felt beholden to fewer still. To one, in fact.

For the first time in his life he felt a twinge of conscience. He never wasted energy on doubt. Never wasted time on wondering. That enabled him to have the necessary focus to complete the high-risk missions he undertook. He'd never questioned any assignment Del had given him. And while the nature of his business allowed a great deal of latitude in how he got the job done, he also never questioned the occasional parameters he was given.

Until now.

It felt wrong. Deep down wrong that both of these people he admired and respected were being deprived of ever knowing each other. Wrong that Blue wouldn't have the chance to know her father, even to know he was alive.

A pretty damn odd thing to feel, for a man who'd never known a single thing about any member of his family, dead or alive.

"I guess you're right," she said finally, then let out a short, self-deprecating laugh. "God knows it's not like I haven't misjudged people in the past."

She swung back around to Tiny. "Mind if I bum your trailer from you? I had a flat out by Stone Mesa."

Tiny sighed deeply and shook his head.

Blue lifted her hand. "No more lectures today,

okay? Just let me use the trailer. Dinner is on the house tonight."

He smiled. "Beer too?"

Now Blue sighed, but she was smiling too. "You're so loyal, Tiny. With friends like you—"

"You get to keep your precious hog from getting sandblasted sitting out in the desert all night," Tiny finished.

She laughed. "True, true. For that alone I ought to offer you free meals for a week." She eyed his belly. "But I won't."

Tiny laughed and wrapped a big, meaty arm around Blue's shoulder. Diego watched them stroll over to the trailer, absently rubbing his palm over his midriff.

The situation had been defused better than he could have hoped for. Especially considering how big the potential for disaster had been.

He had to get Blue back to the cantina, then get on the horn for an update. Jacounda had very definitely located Blue. It was only a matter of time before he sent in another team. He would never know how his team had been taken out or, more importantly, by whom. But he'd know now that Del was actively protecting Blue. The next team wouldn't come in cocky and bold.

Diego's mind began to spin out the various possible scenarios and the corresponding actions he would have to take.

The familiar process did nothing to ease the sudden ache in his chest.

His palm shifted higher, absently seeking out the source of the pain. He looked at Blue, focused on her. The twinge sharpened.

His whole life had been spent walking the perimeter around which others lived. Existing on the fringe was both mandatory to his occupation and a personal choice.

So why did he suddenly feel left out?

Blue dragged out a barstool and slumped onto it, leaning her elbows on the counter and resting her head on her fists. She was exhausted both in body and in mind. Her spirit, however, was strangely energized.

She heard the clanging noises of pots and pans coming from the kitchen, where Diego was still cleaning up after an extraordinarily busy day and night.

The source of her energy. She'd given up denying her fascination with her new cook. Of course, it wasn't every day she found herself attracted to a man who might be trying to kill her.

Her heart said no. Her head said maybe. She'd lost big the last time she'd followed her heart.

She sighed, then took a long pull on the icy beer she'd grabbed from behind the bar. Again and again she'd gone over the day's events, and all that had led up to them. At the time it had all made sense to her. No matter what her instincts told her, it was tough to believe she was in danger when things seemed normal.

On the one hand, it was possible that Diego was

somehow involved in whatever was going on. On the other hand, he might be just what he claimed. A cook.

Besides, she didn't even really know if anything was "going on." She only had Leroy's word on that.

That and two men in a dark sedan. Another in a pickup truck.

And then there was the knife. Or lack of one.

She took another sip, then stilled suddenly, the beer still sitting on her tongue. Very slowly, casually, she straightened her spine and let the beer slide down her throat. She didn't have to look in the mirror behind the bar to know she was no longer alone.

Lord, but the man moved quietly. *Yes, but that doesn't make him a killer.* Oh, shut up already! She wanted to put her hands over her ears and hum. Instead she met his gaze in the mirror. He stood about ten feet behind her. She lifted her bottle. "Beer?"

The impact she felt in just looking at him had only increased, even with all her mental gymnastics. There was nothing overt about him, or how he looked at her. But when he made eye contact with her, it never failed to strike a chord deep within her.

Eye contact was a tool few people understood or used. Blue had always known just how effective it could be. Her father had been a master at it. She'd been trying since she was five to copy it, and though she'd never matched him, she prided herself on her skill.

But it had never been used on her. Not like this. She had no idea what he was after, what he was thinking, what he was feeling. But she doubted he'd intended to elicit the response in her that he did.

And he did. Did he ever.

She had no idea how to react to that. How to protect herself. Yet she had no doubt that protection was necessary.

"That's okay," he said. "You about done out here?"

Blue almost smiled. She liked his quiet brand of concern. Not that he'd ever intimated that she needed it. Quite the opposite. He'd certainly never displayed any macho urges around her. Of any kind.

She stifled the odd sting that brought, chiding herself for letting pride and ego get tangled up in an already too tangled web. Besides, she'd made that mistake already. And mistakes were fine, everyone made them. But she'd thought she was at least smart enough not to repeat them.

She looked at him and knew she wasn't going to be smart.

She liked his checking on her. She liked his quiet voice. She liked the way he looked into her instead of at her.

She liked having him in her personal space. She didn't want him to leave. Not yet.

"Oh, come on," she said easily, almost too easily. The zing of risk only made her push harder. "Just one. You busted your rear tonight and I know how hot it gets back there." He didn't so much as move a muscle, yet she sensed his sudden edginess. She smiled. Maybe she affected him a teeny tiny bit after all.

No, not smart at all. There was risk here.

And fun. How long had it been since she'd taken any chances? Since she'd done anything the least bit dangerous?

Since she'd had any fun?

She caught his gaze and held on to it. He met her challenge easily. Another thrill raced down her spine. "On the house. Boss's orders."

He paused for another endless moment, but she was in no hurry. She felt alive and aware. Had she ever been this much of either?

He dipped his chin in a brief nod. It was all she could do not to let out a sigh of relief. He was staying. It wasn't over yet. She got to continue to ride this wild new wave.

She started to get up, but he motioned her down.

"I can get it. You sit." At her raised brow, he added, "I wasn't the only one on my feet all night."

He'd already taken off his apron. He used his T-shirt to open the tall brown bottle. He stayed on the other side of the bar and leaned back against the register, crossing his ankles and resting his free arm across his stomach.

Blue's own stomach muscles tightened at the sexy picture he made. She avoided his gaze and looked back at her beer bottle. Then, rejecting the self-protective move, she looked at him.

Empty, she decided. If eyes were truly windows to the soul . . . then this man had none.

She tensed against the chill that raced over her skin.

Ignoring the sudden resurgence of her instincts, almost in defiance of them, she smiled at him. "Thank you for getting my bike."

He shrugged. The simple movement of shoulders made her pulse skip. How could she shiver and feel uncomfortably hot all at the same time? She traced the cool beads of moisture running down her beer bottle, and continued to look at him.

"Tiny said you could pick it up tomorrow morning anytime."

She nodded. "Good, then I can get in my practice session."

"Practice?"

"Pistol, rifle, shotgun. Up on Red Rock Mesa."

Had she said it on purpose? She didn't know. Didn't care. She watched him, wondering what she was offering. Wondering if he would take it.

"Why?"

Her fingers paused on the cold, wet glass. "Because there are natural targets up there and it doesn't seem to disturb anything." She didn't know what she'd expected him to ask, but that one-word question was far more complicated than it seemed.

"Why do you shoot at all?"

He wasn't going to let it go. "I was taught as a child, by my father. I seem to have a talent for it. And I enjoy it. The focus it requires helps me clear my head." She laughed. "When I was young I even dreamed about being a biathlete. But I grew up in southern New Mexico. The skiing part was a bit tough to work on down there."

"There are other shooting sports."

Her smile faltered. Biathlete. Police detective. Her dreams had never been taken seriously. At best they'd been seen as unfeminine and unattainable; at worst, too foolish or dangerous. She didn't share her dreams anymore, past or present. Until today.

Only her father had listened and understood. Her father . . . and now Diego Santerra.

"Yes, there are. But I was sparked by the challenge of the racing combined with the sharpshooting. I don't discount the skill required for stationary target shooting, it just didn't call to me."

Like you do. The words echoed in her brain so loudly, she spent a panicked second wondering if she'd voiced them out loud.

He watched her steadily, his expression never changing.

She wanted to sigh in relief, but there was none. The tension between them grew, tightening around her muscles, winding through her body until she had to work not to squirm with it.

"Why didn't you follow through?" he asked. "Skiing isn't that far away, if you'd wanted it badly enough." If he sensed her discomfort, he didn't show it.

She responded to the quiet challenge in his voice, even as she wondered if he'd done it purposely. "My parents divorced when I was seven. I didn't see my father again until I was fifteen. We had only a brief time together, but we shared everything. He was killed shortly after that. Both my parents were." He didn't so much as blink, but she felt his focus on her as if it were a physical jab. Her voice faltered, then dropped to a whisper. "I sort of lost my drive for it after he was gone."

"I'm sorry, Blue." His eyes were so empty, but his words caressed her.

"Did you have a childhood dream you had to give up?" she asked, suddenly needing to know him. "Or one that you gave up on?"

He slowly tilted the bottle to his lips and finished the beer in one long swallow. She watched his throat muscles work, intensely drawn to each minute movement.

Finished, he straightened and set the bottle gently on the counter between them. She felt her breath catch in her throat as he continued to look at her.

"I didn't have a childhood," he said. "I was never a child."

While she searched for the words to say to him, he moved out from behind the bar and went to the front door. What could she say to that?

She watched mutely as he checked the locks on the front door and closed the blinds on the windows. He crossed behind the bar and picked up his bottle. "You done?"

She stared dumbly at her beer for a second, still stunned by his bald declaration, then nodded. He took it by the rim, his fingers touching the glass her lips had dampened only seconds ago. Blue rubbed her hands along her biceps and forearms.

"Lock up behind me." He was at the door to the hallway when she found her voice.

"Diego."

He stopped, but it was a moment before he turned to face her. "Yes?"

There were simply no words for what she wanted to say to him, for the feelings he evoked in her. "You want to come shoot with me in the morning?"

She'd surprised him.

"Think about it," she said quickly, not wanting an outright rejection. Not yet. "Tejo can get me to Tiny's in the morning. I'll probably leave from there around eight."

There was another brief silence. "I'll take you to Tiny's. But we can take the Jeep to the mesa."

"Taking the bike is half the fun. You can follow me if you want." Her smile grew. "If you think you can."

"I'll pick you up around seven-thirty," was all he said. But it was enough. He nodded toward the door. "Follow me back so you can lock up behind me."

He paused by the kitchen to put the bottles in the out crate, then flicked off the light, pitching them in almost total darkness. The light from the bar area cast the hall in deep shadow.

He turned to her at the door, his tall sturdy frame filling the space around them. This was the closest she'd been to him without a bar, desk, or gearshift between them.

"Do you plan on working tonight?" He nodded at her partially open office door.

Blue sighed in disgust. "I should. I'd planned on doing that this morning. But then Gerraro called, and well, you know the story from there. So much for making plans. I really should bag tomorrow morning and do it then, but . . ."

"I know. You have to get out of here, have some time that is all yours. Clear your head."

"Exactly. Today's excursion didn't exactly accomplish that." She smiled. "I need to shoot at something."

"I know that feeling."

Blue heard more than typical compassion in his tone. She hadn't forgotten her suspicions, she just couldn't make herself believe them.

Couldn't . . . or didn't want to.

"You sure you want me there?" he said. "I don't want you to bring your business with you."

Suspicion dulled as excitement thrummed inside her. "I won't be. I'd like you to come."

He didn't move, yet it seemed as if he were closer somehow. He lifted his hand, and her entire body tightened at the expectation of his touch.

But it never came.

Had she just imagined it because she wanted so desperately to feel his touch? She was acutely aware of every inch of him. She felt his breath against her face.

"I'd better get out of here and let you get some sleep then," he said. "I'll see you in the morning."

Sleep. Bed. Diego. Until morning. Blue could no

more stop the images that filtered into her brain than fly to the moon. "Yeah," she finally managed, glad she got the word out at all.

"You going to be okay? Did Gerraro say he'd keep an eye on the place tonight?"

She almost laughed. He'd misread her reaction as fear. There was fear in her, but not of Leroy and his threats. She was afraid she was about to take a step that would take her outside of the closed circle she'd drawn around herself.

"Yes, he did." She took a step, almost closing the spare distance between them. "I'll be just fine," she said quietly. "I always am."

He didn't say anything, and lifted his hand again. It was inches away from her face when he pulled back. She almost whimpered in frustration.

"Good night, Blue."

"Yeah," she whispered, wishing she had the nerve to touch him first. "Night."

Diego pulled his Jeep into Blue's parking lot the following morning and drove around back. He scanned the area, pausing briefly on the small mesa behind the cantina that had served as his bed the night before. John had helped him keep surveillance, trading perimeter checks off and on during the night. Jacounda wouldn't wait long before sending in another team. The trial had begun and Del was scheduled to testify within the week.

He slid out of the truck just as the back door

opened. Blue walked out looking like a female Rambo. She had a soft leather gun case slung over her shoulder, a hard rifle case in one hand, and a smaller pistol attaché in her other. Her hair was tied back in a long single braid, her eyes shaded with dark Ray•Bans. She had a webbed vest on over her army-tan T-shirt, several pockets bulging with shotgun shells and rifle ammo.

"You carry all that on the bike?"

She smiled. "Good morning to you too. And yes, I do."

"I bet you make quite a sight." The understatement of the century. And more than he should have said. He'd agreed to accompany her because it made his job easier. The offer had come at precisely the right time. A gift he wouldn't refuse. Couldn't. Not with things tightening down. Going with her was a hell of a lot easier than tracking her unseen through the wide-open desert.

None of which explained why he'd had to curl his fingers into fists to keep from touching her in that dark hallway the night before. Raging hormones didn't fill in the blank either, though they were certainly all present and accounted for.

This deep-centered need to protect her, to take her into his arms and shield her from any and all harm, that he hadn't explained either.

"I guess I do." Her shrug made it clear she didn't really care what she looked like or what anyone thought of her unusual hobby. "They strap on the back of the bike. I had Tiny make a special rack and bungee webbing."

"I'll follow in the Jeep," was all Diego allowed himself to say.

She stowed her gear in the back of the Jeep, then turned to him and lowered her sunglasses halfway down her nose. "What, you don't trust women drivers?"

He felt blinded. Sunstruck. Her flash of white teeth was as bright as a high-noon sun, her voice velvety and soft like a dark desert night, her eyes blazing hot as the sands.

"Not enough room." Not nearly enough, he thought. Squeezing his body behind hers, wrapping himself around her . . . No, not smart. Definitely not smart.

"If I can take Tiny, I can take you."

Take me. Diego wanted to groan. "I thought Tiny had his own bike."

"He does. But I'm not the only one who's had a flat out there."

"Well, now you won't have to call if you have a flat."

Her smile spilled into a deep chuckle. He felt his entire body respond to that musical sound. Low, and a bit rough.

He wanted to make it rougher.

She slid her glasses back on and crossed her arms over her chest. "Chicken."

Really not smart, Santerra. The corners of his mouth twitched. "You got an extra helmet?"

"Thought you'd never ask." She turned and went back into the cantina. His gaze zeroed in on the perfect fit of her jeans until the door closed behind her, telling himself it was too-long-denied hormones making him desert crazy.

But her incredible body wasn't the source of his fascination and he knew it. It was the inside of the package that had him making stupid decisions. John would take his head off when he saw them on one bike heading hell-bent across the desert. And rightly so. If he didn't pass out from shock.

Diego Santerra didn't make bad decisions. And certainly not ones influenced by personal wants.

Personal wants. When was the last time that he'd had one of those? Since he'd had a need that competed in any way with the job at hand?

The answer was simple. Never. Not once.

He watched the door swing back open and Blue emerge with two bike helmets, one red, one black. He didn't have to ask which one was his. The symbolism didn't escape him.

He knew he should back out, take the truck. There were a dozen ways to do it. Instead he took the black helmet she offered him.

"Let's go," she said.

He walked around to the driver's side of the Jeep, watched her slide onto her seat and buckle in before turning her smile on him once again. It was full of anticipation and pleasure. Because of him. She was happy just to be with him.

He looked at her and felt the same anticipation,

the same pleasure. He knew then why he'd never allowed himself needs, wants.

Because once begun, there would be no end to them.

Not with Blue Delgado.

SIX

They decided to leave the Jeep at Tiny's. Blue cut into the desert at the same spot they'd left it the day before. Diego knew it wasn't the wisest move since Jacounda's men had tracked them from there, but the risk was minimal. The second team wouldn't repeat the first team's plan. And Hermes couldn't get them in place this fast. Besides, John would be out there today to help keep an eye on things.

What would John think if he knew he was also playing chaperon to his partner? And since when did Diego care what other people thought?

Since you started needing a chaperon.

He leaned on the upright hard gun case strapped to the bike, his hands locked behind his hips on the metal gun frame. His hand was closer to his knife this way.

It was also not wrapped around Blue's waist.

He scanned the open area, turning his head

slightly to look back as best he could without drawing undue attention to his actions. He knew Blue could see him from her sideview mirrors. He felt it each and every time she glanced back at him. Where he did not look was down.

The space between his spread thighs and her firm backside was marginal at best. And he did his damnedest to keep it that way. Just as his body did its damnedest to reach out to her anyway.

Being this close and not touching was somehow even more erotically charged. Denial created the most potent temptation.

He focused on the discomfort of not being able to shift in his seat. Used it as proof of his foolishness, as a means to get his head back where it should be.

It wasn't working.

Blue lifted her hand and pointed to a tumble of rock about a mile ahead. One large mesa rose from the middle, blazing red in the early-morning sun. Red Rock Mesa.

She slowed the bike, turning her head slightly, shouting to be heard over the whine of the engine.

"Pull your knees in. There is a path to the top, but we have to squeeze through some tight spots to get to it."

She leaned in around a tumble of rocks then headed straight for what looked like a solid stone wall. Only when they were about ten yards away did Diego see the angled alley. He pulled his knees in, pressing them against her thighs.

Just as they approached she slowed even more, her shout traveling more clearly this time.

"Lean into me. I need to keep our weight more centered through here."

Diego really wanted to be in his Jeep.

He curved his shoulders in, the breadth of them just framing hers. The curve of his face shield forced him to tuck his head on one side of hers. In order to keep his balance, he had to close the distance between them.

And let go of the metal frame.

His chest brushed her back as he carefully placed one hand, then the other, on her hips. He felt her tense against his body.

A hot flush stole over him. He wasn't the only one going on sensory overload. He scoped out the tumble of rocks and boulders as Blue skillfully—and excruciatingly slowly—wove her way through them. They were going just fast enough to keep her from having to put her foot on the ground for balance.

The rise of the buttes blocked out a good part of the sun, creating shadows around the towering boulders. A sniper's paradise.

Diego was so alert, his nerves were almost screaming. And being wrapped around Blue only heightened his senses.

"Almost there," she yelled.

She turned the bike and they slid through another invisible slit in the rock, then popped out into the bright sun.

"Hold on!"

He barely had time to grip her hips and press his thighs tighter when she made an almost hairpin turn, sending them up a winding path. When he looked up, they were climbing Red Rock Mesa. There might be another route to the top that could carry a Jeep, but not this one. This was Blue's track—one rut, two wheels, in line.

The bike rumbled and shook, the back tire sliding out a bit on the loose rock. But they moved together, balanced, in sync, as if they'd learned each other's rhythms long ago.

By the time Blue rounded the last turn and gunned the engine, shooting them onto the flat open top of the mesa, Diego wasn't sure he could move away from her. Much less climb off the bike and walk.

She slowed to a stop, placing her feet on the ground, and balancing the bike between her thighs. Diego had to swallow an involuntary groan as she leaned forward, grinding her backside into his groin.

She flicked the chin strap open and pulled off her helmet, turning to look at him. "You'll have to slide off first. I'll balance the bike. Just watch out for the exhaust pipes."

He didn't say anything. He also didn't move. Her face was backlit by the morning sun, casting her dark eyes into even deeper shadows, accentuating the almost regal slant of her cheekbones, the strong line of her nose. Behind his tinted visor, his gaze dropped to her mouth.

Voluptuous was the word that sprang to mind. He wanted to kiss that mouth, softly and deeply. He wanted to sink his lips onto hers, slide his tongue against them, taste them, part them. Luxuriate in the contrast of her silken lips and the slightly rougher texture of her tongue. He thought of how she would taste at first . . . then later when her tongue mingled with his.

His fingers curled inward, and he realized he was still holding her hips. A little half moan escaped her lips and he immediately released her. The moan became a sound of protest.

He stilled, his hands only an inch away from touching her.

She reached up and lifted his visor.

He looked into her eyes. "Blue." He wasn't sure if it was a plea or a warning. "I shouldn't do this."

"Do what?"

"Kiss you."

"Oh." The word was a sigh. "Why?"

"Because you're business. And all I can see right now is pleasure."

"You mean because you're my cook?"

Because that's not all I am. "Yes."

"I know you don't know me that well, but I don't mix the two, Diego. This isn't about your job, no matter what happens. Or doesn't."

"Then what is it about?" He didn't realize how badly he needed an answer to that question until he asked it. "What are we doing here?"

Her eyes clouded a bit and her voice softened. "I don't know."

He felt her confusion. Nothing was simple anymore. There was so much she didn't know. Couldn't know.

"I've never done this," she added.

He let his hands rest on his thighs. "Then let's not start now."

He slid off the bike before he couldn't. His back to her, he pulled off his helmet and scanned the horizon, wondering where John was. Wondering when Jacounda would try again.

He heard her flick out the kickstand. Straps snapped off and he knew she was unpacking her guns.

The irony that he'd been protecting a sharp-shooter with a knife hadn't escaped him. She hadn't come up here in the time he'd been watching her, but he'd known about her target practices. Del's dossier on his daughter hadn't included the reason for them, though. Her aborted dreams of being an athlete. He wondered if Seve knew she still yearned, still dreamed, whether it be biathlete or police officer. He wondered if his boss knew his disappearance from Blue's life had caused her to change her path so greatly.

"Do you want to shoot? Or watch?"

He turned to find her twenty yards away, setting up her targets. He recognized the targets as the same ones used by professional shooters. He imagined they were Olympic standard issue.

"Watch." He wasn't sure he could miss convincingly.

She walked back to the gun cases. Squatting, she turned the hard case on its side and opened it. Inside was the most beautiful .22-caliber rifle Diego had ever seen.

"Quite a piece you have there."

She smiled; her expression held both pride and wistfulness. "It was my father's. He had it altered to Olympic specs."

Diego masked his sudden frustration. "That's some legacy."

She looked up, squinting against the sun. "You mean a father shouldn't share something like guns with his daughter?"

"I was sincere. You're lucky to have something of his that was special to both of you."

"I'm sorry. That was rude of me." She looked back at him. "Thank you."

She spoke almost reverently about her father. At any other time of his life, he might have questioned how they had bonded so intensely in so short a period of time. Not now.

He held her gaze for a second. "You're welcome, Blue."

She turned her attention back to the rifle. After checking over the gun, she slipped the leather sling over her head to rest on one shoulder and stood.

She walked a couple of steps away and turned to face her targets, sliding in a five-bullet clip and chambering the first round. Diego watched her, taking periodic visual sweeps of the desert floor below them. On the one hand, being up there gave him the advantage of seeing the enemy approach. On the other, if they got past him and John and made it as far as the boulders, sound would be the only sense he could rely on.

"What about you?"

Her question startled him from his thoughts. She was standing stock-still, rifle balanced perfectly on her shoulder, eyeing down the peep sight. The rifle had no scope and a smaller clip, probably only a few of the modifications Del had made to the gun.

"What about me what?" he asked.

The rifle jerked as she shot the first round. The small metal disk on the left end of the row spun around, then settled back on its base.

Without moving, she examined her target, then chambered another round and prepared to shoot again. She wasted no motion, moving with the grace and ease of someone long familiar with the task at hand. Diego identified closely with that connection.

"Don't you have anything special from your parents? Your family?" She concentrated on the next target as she spoke.

"No."

She lowered the rifle without shooting and turned to face him.

"Nothing?"

"Nothing."

"Not sentimental?"

He shook his head. "No family."

"None? Not ever?" She quickly lifted her hand. "I'm sorry, this is none of my business. I should have known from what you said yesterday, in the bar."

"It's okay."

"No, it's not. But I didn't mean to pry."

"I know." And he did. Maybe that was why he'd answered her at all. Not that he'd said that much, but it was more than he'd ever revealed to anyone. Except her father. Del was the only person who knew his whole story.

The silence stretched out for several seconds, before she turned and lifted the rifle to her shoulder again. He watched as she centered herself and steadied the gun. He stood as stock-still as she did when she pulled the trigger a second time. An instant later the second target spun on its pole.

"Do you ski?"

She paused in the middle of reloading to look at him. "Ski?"

He nodded at the targets. "You're good at shooting. Very good. I was just wondering if you'd ever done the skiing part."

She glanced away with a smile, a bit of heat in her cheeks. Diego felt the breath leave his chest.

"Not once. Never even had them strapped to my feet." She laughed. "A biathlete wannabe who's never skied. Pretty funny, isn't it?"

He walked over to her, drawn to her in ways that went way past the physical.

"You want to know something even funnier?" Her hand rubbed the stock of her gun, giving away her nervousness.

He didn't want her to be uneasy. He wanted her to feel natural, to be able to say anything to him. He wanted her willing to share herself with him.

But sharing was not a one-way proposition.

And the discovery that the idea of sharing himself in return wasn't terrifying shook him up more than anything else.

"What's funnier?" he asked.

She laughed, the sound soft, but self-deprecating. "I've never even seen snow. Not for real."

"Never seen snow?"

She shook her head. "Pretty hysterical, isn't it?"

"Why?"

She caught his gaze as if gauging how much more of herself she should reveal.

All of it, he wanted to say, shocking himself again with the strength and sureness of the response.

"Why not, Blue? Never had the chance? Never made the chance?"

"Never made the chance." It was an admission.

"Why?"

She looked away. His hand was on her cheek before he realized he'd moved, turning her face back to his. "Tell me the rest."

She stared at him. "I have no idea why I told you what I have."

His touch turned into a caress. "I'm not sure why I need to know, either. But I do know one thing."

"What?"

"You can tell me anything."

She started to turn away, but he held her chin, gently keeping her face tilted to his. He waited for her to look at him again.

"And anything you do tell me is safe with me." He

slid his fingers back, cupping her head. "You are safe with me."

"Diego."

He tilted her head back, lowering his mouth to hers. An inch away from tasting her, she closed her hand around his forearm.

"There is no such thing as safety," she whispered, her breath caressing his lips.

He stared into her eyes, feeling his heart race. "Maybe not," he admitted. "But there is calculated risk."

"I'm not sure I'm ready to risk anything again."

"There are no guarantees in life, Blue. Just take things as they come. No rules. No expectations."

"No promises."

"I only make promises I can keep. I haven't broken one yet."

"How many have you made?"

His mouth curved at the corners. Smart woman. "Very few."

"Fair enough."

He framed her face with his other hand, letting his thumbs drift over her lower lip. He felt her slight tremor race through his fingers all the way to his toes. "Can I taste you now?" He'd meant to sound cocky, but his voice sounded needy. Too needy.

Her lips were parted under the pressure of his thumb. And when he brushed the pad over the edge of her teeth she moaned deep in her throat.

He paused, searching her eyes, for what, he didn't know.

She let go of the rifle, letting it dangle on her hip from the sling, and cupped his face, catching him badly off guard.

Touching her was wreaking havoc on him, but he was unprepared for her touching him. He'd never gotten that far in his mind. Had never known being touched could be like this. Dangerous.

"No rules, right?" she asked, a smile playing at the corners of her mouth.

His fingertips followed the curve of her lips.

She did the same to him.

"No," he said, his voice no more than a rasp. "No, there aren't."

"Kiss me, Diego."

Never stop touching me, Blue. The sweet pressure of her lips under his was the only way he could be sure he hadn't spoken out loud. He deepened the kiss, feeling her lips getting wet and slippery with the taste of him . . . of them.

"Touch me, Blue."

His roughly murmured plea was answered immediately. She slid her tongue into his mouth, and pushed her fingers into his hair, down his neck, then across his shoulders.

He shuddered and took her tongue into his mouth, holding her there as he wanted her to hold him. Inside her. Deeply. Tightly.

She skimmed her hands down to the small of his back, pressing her palms against him, urging his body forward. If he so much as brushed against her, he knew he would spontaneously combust.

He pulled his lips from hers, almost moaning at the sudden emptiness he felt without her tongue filling his mouth. He rested his forehead on hers, catching his breath, listening to hers even out as well. Her hands relaxed on his back.

He lifted his head and looked into her eyes. She met his gaze easily, and held it.

He'd never felt so evenly matched. He'd never even thought it possible.

And his match was Seve Delgado's daughter. What in the hell was he doing?

"I think maybe we should head back to the cantina," she said, her voice still rough with need. He heard the tremors, felt them.

He stepped back while he could, breaking contact. It felt wrong. "Yeah, maybe we should."

In silence, Diego dismantled her targets while she took care of her rifle and packed it. They both stored the gear on the bike, but neither of them climbed on. Wrapping his body around her was a bad idea, but something he wanted desperately.

He never wanted anything. Desperately or otherwise.

But it was climb on or walk to the cantina. And he could hardly do his job on foot out in the desert.

"After you," he said.

She turned to him. "Have you ever driven one?"

"Not like this one, but yes."

"Have a license?"

"Yes."

She held out the key. "You wanna?"

Oh, yes I do, Blue Delgado. I wanna. A lot.

Even as he took the keys he knew it meant feeling her wrapped around him. Exquisite torture. He told himself that being the driver gave him more control over any potential threat. But the only threat he felt at that moment was her long leg sliding over the seat behind him and her long elegant fingers pressing into his waist.

They were halfway down Red Rock when Diego finally loosened up enough to enjoy the ride and the bike. The woman behind him was another matter entirely.

She tightened her thighs against his as he wove through the narrow passageway, out of the boulder field and into the bright, wide-open desert.

Diego brought the bike to a stop, balancing the heavy machine between his thighs. He flipped up his visor and turned back. "Your turn."

"You can keep on."

"I didn't really follow the track out here." That wasn't exactly a lie. He hadn't wasted time memorizing her route. He knew where they were and where the highway was and several points where John would be in between.

She looked at him for a moment, then shrugged. "Okay." She used his shoulder for balance as she climbed off. Between her hand and the feel of her leg rubbing across his backside, he wasn't sure he could handle her sliding back on in front of him and still be responsible for his actions.

He purposely leaned back and scanned the horizon. Nothing. Still, his instincts had made him stop. Blue could handle the bike as well as he could. Better for him to be behind her, shielding her, protecting her.

He held her hips in a loose but firm grip, keeping the space between them minimal. His reaction was too strong, not to mention highly unprofessional. By kissing her up on the mesa, he'd broken not only a personal code, but a professional one as well. Many men in his line of work relaxed those rules. But not Diego.

Not any of Del's team.

And sure as hell not with Del's daughter.

She flipped the starter, then gunned the engine. The bike roared back to life. Diego kept a close scrutiny on his surroundings as she whipped them across the sands. Something wasn't right. He could feel it.

That his instincts were still functioning did little to relieve him. It wasn't too late, but he had to back off. Now. Focus on keeping her safe.

Not keeping her.

Blue pointed to a truck cutting across the desert, off the track, flying hell-bent for leather. Straight for them.

Diego recognized it immediately. McShane's 4X4. Adrenaline shot into his bloodstream like a needle in a vein. He quickly scanned the horizon. Nothing.

He lifted his visor and yelled to Blue. "Head for the truck."

"More friends of yours?" she shouted back.

He didn't answer, just flipped his visor down and

moved his body closer to hers, his fingers tightening on her hips. He could feel her thighs tense between his knees and knew she felt his anxiety. He continued to look for whatever had sent McShane out of hiding. It had to be Jacounda. But where?

He felt her hunker down and gun it. Good instincts, Blue.

Suddenly McShane changed direction, heading diagonally to their right. Diego immediately looked behind the truck, but as the dust trails settled he saw nothing behind John. Still, the move had been both a defensive maneuver and a signal not to head directly for the truck. But where?

He leaned forward again, yelling over the whine of the engine. "Forget the truck. Take the most direct route to the highway."

To his relief, and to her credit, she didn't ask questions, just angled the bike in a smooth arc toward the highway. The questions, he knew, would come later.

He'd worry about them then. Now he had to get her off the sand and tucked away.

The bang that suddenly echoed behind them was loud enough to jerk Blue. The bike wavered a bit but she didn't lose control. "Just keep on. Go, go, go," Diego shouted.

Blue did as he asked. Diego turned back, braced for what he suspected had happened. He let out a silent sigh of relief, even as he mentally swore. The 4X4 wasn't a ball of flames, but it had been rendered immobile. They were too far away for him to see exactly what had happened. But the smoke and flames shooting out from under the hood and the lopsided tilt to the frame gave him a pretty good idea.

McShane was too good an agent to allow a bomb to be planted anywhere on his vehicle. Which meant Jacounda's men were out here. In the desert.

"What in the hell is going on, Santerra?" she yelled. Her entire body was like a live wire between his thighs.

"Open it up, Blue. Get us on that highway. Then head for Tiny's." He needed his Jeep. His radio.

"What happened back there?" She hadn't turned around to look. "Tell me."

If the situation wasn't so critical, he'd have smiled. Still the boss.

Not out here. And he was no longer just the cook. "Not sure. Just don't slow down until I tell you to."

She turned her head, but her helmet kept her from looking at him. "Why should I listen to you?"

The bike suddenly jerked hard to the right. What the hell? If he hadn't been locked to her, he might have lost his balance, possibly causing her to lose control of the bike. Had she done it on purpose?

She kept their balance and he quickly realized what had happened. They'd hit a rock or something. Another flat tire.

"Keep going," he shouted.

"My frame will be shot," she hollered back.

"Just do it." Diego's mind raced. He knew the sand would cushion the deflating tire somewhat, but it was already slowing them down. The asphalt highway would shred it. He could only hope there would be someone on the road. Commandeering a civilian vehicle was the least of his worries right now. He saw the black strip of highway, barely five hundred yards ahead.

Just then he felt a hot sting streak across his left thigh. He glanced down and saw the graze mark on his jeans. The next shot hit him in the left shoulder, taking him sideways off the bike.

He hit the sand in a roll, rocks and debris cutting at him.

He tumbled to a stop and immediately pushed up on his good arm to look for Blue.

He located her almost immediately. Just in time to see a dusty red pickup swerve off the highway directly in front of her. She slid the bike on its side.

Her name locked in his throat.

Two men jumped out of the back and hauled the bike off her. Her struggle as they hauled her into the cab of the truck was the only indication that she was okay.

Then they drove off with her.

SEVEN

Blue sat as still as possible. Her back was bruised and sore from bouncing against the metal truck bed. Her wrists were raw from the wet bandanna binding them together. At least she had on boots, so her ankles hadn't suffered the same abrasions. Her jaw ached from the other bandanna, wedged back into her molars and tied around her head. Her eyes remained disturbingly uncovered.

Seeing one's abductors was not supposed to be a good thing. She'd scrutinized a half-dozen of them so far. Not one of them looked familiar. And other than Leroy's dire warning, she had no idea why she'd been taken. Of course, that Leroy's warning was apparently well-founded did nothing to console her now.

She glared steadily at the door. Not that she could see the door, only the dim glow that crept in the crack at the bottom. Her abductors hadn't bothered her in hours. Or what felt like hours. As far as she could tell, there were no windows in the room and no furniture either. They'd shoved her roughly into one corner, ordered her to sit, told her not to move, then left her in the dark.

She'd spent most of her time in the corner going over what had happened second by second. Goose-flesh crawled over her skin. She swore under her breath. She couldn't even rub her own arms for comfort.

She held on to her anger by a thread. It was either that or give in to the hysteria that was lodged in a thick ball at the base of her throat.

Diego was the one who had put her back in front as the driver. Diego was the one who said he recognized the truck. Diego had ordered her to head for the highway. And her abductors.

Most damning of all, Diego had bailed off the bike, leaving her to face her fate alone. Apparently his job had been completed.

Killer or mere accomplice, he was guilty in her book.

And she'd let the bastard kiss her! The absolute worst part of all was that she'd enjoyed it. Would have pushed further if he hadn't stopped them. And she knew he'd been completely aware of that. She'd thought he was dancing on that same fine edge as well. His control and his calm words had made her feel secure. False security.

It wasn't about control and caring. He'd had an appointment to keep!

She had no idea what was going to happen to her,

but she knew she should be formulating some sort of plan. She had to get out of here alive. If only to hunt down her son-of-a-bitching cook and kill him. Right after she fired him.

The door suddenly burst open. She squinted against the bright light just as a blinding flash went off mere feet from her eyes. A camera?

Then hands came out of the darkness and grabbed the back of her head. She immediately began to fight.

"Sit still!" The voice was deep and unrecognizable.

The bandanna dropped away from her mouth and pain rushed in as she carefully tried to work her jaw. Then someone jerked her face around, straining her neck, until she was staring into a pair of tiny black eyes set in a wide, smooth face.

He shoved a small recorder to her mouth. "State your name."

She blinked at him, pain still vibrating through her face.

"Your full name. Say it!"

The command somehow snapped her back into focus. No more blindly following commands. "Why?"

His fingers tightened cruelly on her jaw. She winced involuntarily.

"Say it, or I make you say it."

Blue debated the merits of pushing the big man. "Blue."

"Full name."

"Delgado."

He shoved her face away, the force snapping her head back against the wall. She glared at the retreating hulk as the door slammed and she was once again in the dark. Another person on her hit list.

At least he'd left the bandanna off.

With a sigh that ended on a soft moan, she gently leaned her bruised head back against the wall. It was time to find a way out of here. One thing she'd learned about herself during her divorce was that she was far from helpless.

She dug her heels in and scooted her bottom forward. Progress was slow. The hardwood floor made sliding easy, but moving more forward than backward was tough. Staying close to the wall, she crawled around the perimeter of the room, hoping to find something, anything, that might help her escape. She hadn't encountered so much as an electrical cord.

She rounded the corner to the wall containing the door, making as little noise as possible. Just as she slid in front of the doorjamb, voices erupted on the other side.

"He'll still testify. That picture won't stop him. He hasn't seen her in years."

"We've got her saying her name on tape."

Blue heard swearing accompanied by a brief thud of flesh hitting flesh.

"Hey!" It was the second voice.

"That could be anyone, you moron. I'm telling you, you could get her saying it on the six o'clock news and he'll still testify."

"Well, you'd better pray you're wrong. Señor

Jacounda is counting on her being his ticket out. Mr. Super Spy utters one word on the stand next week, and we're dead."

Blue's mind was spinning. She had no idea what they were talking about.

A tiny scratching sound caught her attention. She squinted into the darkness but saw nothing. Mice?

Just then a circle popped out of the wall next to her. When moonlight flooded in, she realized it had come from a windowpane. A blacked-out window. She'd scooted around the entire room and the one and only window had been less than three feet away from her starting point.

A hand reached in and up, silently releasing the lock. Blue slid backward as far and fast as she dared go, pushing herself into the opposite corner. She had no idea who was coming in the room, but since she still had no idea who the bad guys were, it was impossible to determine who the good guys were either.

In fact, she'd have to say at the moment there were no good guys.

The moon shadowed the large shape of a man sliding noiselessly into the room. If her heart hadn't been pounding so loudly, she might have been more impressed by his grace.

"Blue."

His whisper was rough and low. She froze, but remained silent.

"It's okay. I'm here to get you out."

Yeah, right. Someone she didn't know wanted her

dead and now someone else she didn't know wanted to rescue her. Who were these people?

"If you can't talk, tap the floor lightly." His voice was like velvet, just reaching her ears, like a caress.

"I don't want to move any more than necessary or use any light. Just point me in the right direction and I'll have you out of here."

Well, getting out at the very least opened up more escape possibilities.

"Who are you?" she whispered.

In one rapid heartbeat, he knelt in front of her. "John McShane."

"And why are you rescuing me, John McShane? Who do you work for?"

"A distant relative of Uncle Sam. Come on, we can do this later." He shifted again. "How are you tied?"

Blue felt grudging gratitude for the man. He could have just manhandled her, and she'd had quite enough of that.

"My hands behind my back and my ankles. The bandannas are wet, so it will be hard to—"

She felt a slight pressure, then her hands were released. A second later the bonds fell away from her ankles.

"You must have been one helluva Boy Scout."

"Not in this lifetime." She heard the grin in his voice. "But knives do come in handy."

Blue stiffened. Images of Leroy flashed through her mind. "Knife?"

"Yeah. Don't normally use them. I'm holding on

to this one for a friend," McShane went on, talking over her sudden anxiety. "Can you stand?" He rose before her. "Give me your hand. Just don't make any sound."

Blue again gave silent thanks for his consideration in not grabbing at her to help her up. She felt brutalized and fragile and didn't like either feeling the least bit. He was handing her back her freedom along with a sense of control. She liked John McShane.

She just hoped he hadn't been sent there to kill her.

"Here." She raised both hands and instantly felt his slide across hers. His touch was cool and impersonal.

"Let's move."

Her shoulders and legs screamed in protest. She had to bite down on her lower lip to keep from groaning, but less than a minute later they were out of the window and crouched on the ground. John's voice just reached her ear. "There are dogs and guards. Stay low and follow me. If I stop, you stop. When I move, you move. The Jeep is in front of us at about two o'clock. When we get there, climb in and stay down."

Only one person she knew drove a Jeep. Diego. And then there was the knife. John had said he was holding it for a friend. She thought of the empty sheath on Diego's waistband. Had these two been involved in what had happened to Leroy? And if they had, how were they involved with the men inside this house?

Her mind spinning, Blue didn't move when

McShane did. He backed up and she heard a sharp, "Now."

She did know that she couldn't stay there. At least in the Jeep she had a fighting chance. She moved.

They reached the dark green truck without incident. He pushed her inside and down, leaving her little time to examine the vehicle. But she was fairly certain it was Diego's.

"Stay as low as you can."

Blue squatted half on the seat, half on the floor.

McShane started the Jeep, kept the lights off, and moved forward at a slow pace. Blue wanted to scream at him to floor it, but he'd gotten them this far, so she kept her mouth shut.

Between her pounding heart and wired nervous system, it was all Blue could do to focus her thoughts. Who was John McShane? He'd said he worked for a distant relative of Uncle Sam. An agent for some spook organization maybe? She would have laughed at her men's-adventure-novel-like thinking, but she was afraid she might actually be right. And how did he tie in to Diego?

She tried to remember what the men in the house had been saying, but McShane's surprise entrance had pushed the conversation completely out of her mind.

"You can get up now."

Blue lifted her head. It was pitch-dark, the moon high. She figured at least midnight or shortly after. She carefully pulled herself onto the seat, biting her lip to keep from making any sound. With the adrenaline rush subsiding, her ankles, arms, and shoulders ached from her hours spent in restraints. Out of habit, she pulled the seat belt across her chest. A short laugh escaped her before she could stop it.

"Glad to hear someone is finding something amusing in all this."

She turned to look at her new captor. Although she wasn't exactly being held captive, her only other option at the moment was to dive out the open door of a moving Jeep.

"I just thought it was funny to worry about highway safety when in all likelihood you plan on leaving my body out in the desert somewhere."

He shot her a look then turned his attention back to the highway. "Why would you think that? I just rescued you."

"Well, it seems to me I've just traded one captor for another."

"You're not a captive."

"Fine, then. Thank you for your help. You can stop the Jeep and let me out."

He glanced at her again, but didn't say anything.

"That's what I thought."

Blue studied him in the dim light. He was tall, rangy. His hair looked light, but not true blond. It was hard to tell. She looked back at the road, berating herself for not paying attention to her surroundings.

"You're not a captive. You're in protective custody."

"Whose providing the protection?"

"Uncle Sam."

"You said that before. Who exactly do you work for?"

"I'm not at liberty to say. But until it's safe to go back to Villa Roja, you'll be under protection."

Villa Roja. Tejo! In all the turmoil she'd forgotten her uncle. "I need to contact my uncle, let him know I'm okay."

"He's been contacted. He knows you're safe."

She snorted. "Then he knows more than I do."

"You're under our protection," he repeated.

"What if I don't want it? And who does have the liberty to say? I'm not entirely sure, but I have some basic civil rights in this, don't I?"

She barely registered that they had left the highway and were climbing into the foothills of the Sangre de Cristo Mountains.

"You have the right to get out now and get yourself killed, or stay with me and live. It will all be explained to you eventually."

Blue crossed her arms and stared out the window. They wound around the narrow roads, moving higher and deeper into the range. Several minutes later McShane turned the Jeep onto a long gravel driveway. Tucked high in hills, the road ended in a clearing. A small cabin was nestled at the far side of it, backing up into the tall trees. He parked in front.

"Don't get any ideas of running off. This is your best chance of survival."

"From what?" Blue finally caved under the pressure. "What exactly is going on? Why are people abducting me? Who wants to kill me? I demand some answers!"

"Or what?"

The deep voice came from behind her. Blue whirled around to find Diego standing several feet away, just off the small front porch. The sling on his arm glowed white in the moonlight.

"What happened to you?" Her head was throbbing. This was too much to assimilate. "Hurt your arm jumping off my bike?"

"He got shot trying to protect your ass," came McShane's sharp retort. With a weary sigh, John walked past Diego. "And while it's a nice one, *amigo*, it's most definitely all yours. I'm done playing white knight. I'm going on first rotation. I'll be back in three hours."

He disappeared around the side of the house, not waiting for a response.

"Come on, let's get inside." Diego sounded weary too.

Blue wasn't inclined to feel sorry for either of them at the moment. "You got shot? Why? By who?"

"Whom. Let's get inside," he repeated, turning back, but waiting for her to precede him.

Blue didn't budge. "Will you explain to me what is going on?"

Diego sighed.

"I'm sorry if my questions are so damn bothersome, but I'm just a little confused. I've been abducted, tied up, rescued, reabducted. I have an old employee telling me I'm going to be killed, a new employee getting shot over it. And whatever is going on is important enough, apparently, for the government to get involved. So you'll just have to excuse me if I'm a little curious."

Diego walked over to her. He was limping. "I'm sorry."

Blue didn't like how his soft declaration made her feel. "Sorry won't cut it," she said, but the sting in her words didn't hold up. She looked up at him. "I just want an explanation. Is that so unreasonable?"

He shook his head. "No. But there are things involved here that you are better off not knowing and that I'm not at—"

"Liberty to discuss," she finished, and sighed in disgust. "Listen, I'm really getting—"

He cut her off. "I promise to tell you what I can. But I'd rather do it inside."

"I thought you didn't make promises." She couldn't stop the memory of his kiss from invading her mind. Her gaze dropped to his mouth. His sharp inhalation brought it quickly back to his eyes.

"Only the ones I can keep."

Blue looked at him for several seconds, then let out a deep breath. "Fine, okay. Let's go inside." She started to walk past him, but he stopped her with a hand on her upper arm.

As soon as she stopped, he let her go. She wasn't sure why the loss of contact bothered her. And she definitely didn't examine the sudden overwhelming need she had to turn to him. To ask him to hold her.

"Are you okay? Did they hurt you, Blue?"

The quiet concern in his voice made her knees soften. She almost gave in to the urge to lean against him.

"I'm okay, all things considered." She nodded at his arm. "You're the one who took the beating."

He said nothing, but neither of them moved. She stood there listening to his level breathing, feeling the sheer strength of him. How could cold, rational doubt fill her mind at the same time determined trust grew inside her heart? Hadn't she learned that lesson?

But then Diego Santerra wasn't Anthony. Far from it. And her response to him couldn't be easily categorized or explained, much less compared with anything she'd ever felt before.

The air between them filled with an energy that was palpable.

He raised his good hand, but let it drop without touching her. She swallowed her disappointment.

"Come on. I need to get off this leg."

She looked down at his legs. He was wearing jeans, and there was no outward sign of injury. But the limp had been obvious.

"From the fall?"

"Sort of." He motioned her ahead of him. She noticed how his gaze swept the area, realizing he'd done that before when they'd been on the mountain. Her step faltered. Had that been only the previous morning? At least a lifetime had transpired since then.

She dropped back to his side. "Do you need help?"

"I'm fine."

She purposely matched his pace. He tried to keep her angled in front of him, but eventually gave up and quickened their pace until they were at the door to the cabin.

She turned just as he reached past her for the door.

"Will they find us up here?" she asked. A small smile surfaced. "Whoever the hell 'they' is."

"I don't think so."

"A strong no would make me feel better."

"I'm trying to keep you alive, but I won't lie to you." He turned the handle and pushed the door open a crack. This time she stopped him with a hand on his arm. He felt warm, solid, strong. And it made her feel protected.

"Thank you for that. Honesty means more to me than just about anything else. And thank you for getting me out of there."

"Don't thank me, thank McShane."

"I don't think he wants to hear from me at this point."

Concern etched his face, but his voice held some warmth. "What did you do to him anyway? Boss him around? He usually enjoys getting beautiful damsels out of distress."

Blue knew she more closely resembled a desert rat at this point than a fairy-tale damsel, so she ignored the obvious compliment. "I was only trying to get some answers. He's about as chatty as you are. And I didn't boss him around. But then, he doesn't work for me."

"Does that mean I'm not fired?"

She smiled. "I don't know. I do know you're not exactly 'just a cook.' " She sobered. "What are you? *Who* are you, Diego Santerra?"

Diego looked into her eyes and had no idea how to answer her. Such a simple question, without one easy answer. "I'm just a man doing his job." Which pretty much summed it up. A man doing his job. No less.

And no more.

He watched Blue sigh, push the door open, and enter the cabin he was going to have to convince her to stay in for the next two weeks without explaining why. Yep. Just doing his job.

The radio gear was gone. McShane must have come in through the back door and taken it with him. Good, thought Diego, locking the front door and double-checking the one on the rear door. Let John deal with the rest of the team. Diego had a feeling his hands would be quite full this evening.

Blue turned around once, took in the small living area, stone fireplace, open kitchen, stairs to the loft bedroom, and the closed door to the lower one, then faced him again.

"Okay, explain."

"A shame you can't get to the point once in a while."

"I know. People love that about me. Why am I here, Diego, and who are you working for?" She held up her hand. "And don't feed me that lame Uncle Sam stuff. It's my life in jeopardy and I think I at least have a right to know who wants me dead and who wants to protect me and why."

"You want something to drink?"

She sighed heavily. "I want some answers."

Stalling was not one of Diego's finer points either. Keeping his mouth shut was.

He gestured to the simple plaid couch that fronted the fireplace. "Why don't you sit down. I'm going to get some coffee. You want some?"

"Sure, fine. I can't drag it out of you. Do whatever you need to do." She sat down, crossed her legs, and folded her arms.

Diego made his way slowly to the kitchen. His thigh was throbbing. His own stupid fault. He'd been pacing the cabin like a wild animal waiting for McShane to get back with Blue. He and McShane had almost come to blows over his insistence on going along to rescue Blue. McShane had cut that off by threatening to tell Del the one or two minor details on the desert incident that Diego had purposely omitted. Like getting shot. They both knew that Del would pull him off the case. If Diego felt he couldn't do the job, he would have withdrawn anyway. But he and John had discussed it, rather loudly at times, and by the end they had agreed. John would get Blue. Diego would contact Tejo and explain what was going on.

He wasn't looking forward to telling Blue about that either.

He popped a few ibuprofens—the other painkillers dulled his reaction time too much—made two mugs of coffee, and returned to the living room. To her credit, Blue didn't pounce until he was seated with his foot propped up.

"Who is trying to kill me?" She made a short, helpless gesture with her hands. "I can't believe I'm even sitting here, up in the mountains in some godforsaken cabin, talking about murderers and people testifying and—"

"What do you know about testifying?" His sharp question grabbed her full attention. "What, Blue? What did they say to you?"

"They, meaning my abductors?"

He nodded.

"Nothing to me directly. I overheard them talking. I also saw several of them. I can describe them. In great detail."

"That's not important right now." Diego knew that as soon as Jacounda discovered he'd failed again, those faces would cease to exist, so trying to match names to faces would be a waste of time.

"I can identify the men who abducted me, but that's not important?"

"What did they say, Blue? What did you hear?" He had to know what information she had before he offered up any of his own.

She swore under her breath, but thankfully didn't push the argument further. "I was tied up and put in a dark room. I was inching around the walls, trying to determine how big the room was and if there were any other doors or windows. When I got by the door I heard them talking. Arguing, actually. Over the picture."

"What picture?" Diego raised his hand. "Wait, wait. Why don't you tell me, one step at a time, what happened."

"I thought you were supposed to answer my questions."

Diego reined in his frustration. Didn't she know how badly it was killing him to do nothing while Jacounda was out there with unlimited resources and men, scheming up another attempt to snatch her?

"I want to keep you safe. I need to know what was said. What you heard."

She shot off the couch. "Why?" she demanded, her voice rising. "Just answer me that one simple question, Diego. Why do you want to keep me safe?"

Diego pushed to a stand, ignoring the dagger of pain shooting up his thigh. "Because that's what I'm paid to do." He leaned forward intending to shift his weight to his good leg, but his thigh cramped, causing him to pitch forward. Blue caught him by the upper arms, but she was off balance as well and the momentum of his weight sent them back onto the couch.

He landed heavily on top of her. He groaned when his shoulder connected with the arm of the couch. She swore.

He tried to roll off of her at the same time she tried to move him.

He groaned again and she stilled. "Wait, wait," she said, the words forced out on a short breath. He was crushing her. "Don't hurt yourself." She grunted and tried to shift her hand out from between them. "Just move your leg and—"

Diego lifted his head and her words died. His face was less than two inches from hers. He managed to drag his good arm free and lever most of his weight off of her, which pressed his lower body intimately between Blue's legs. A fact her suddenly dilating pupils told him she hadn't missed.

"Diego," she whispered.

"I don't want you hurt, Blue." Her lips parted and he swallowed hard against the desire to taste her just one more time.

"It's not just about the job," he heard himself admit. "I don't want to hurt you either. What happened up on Red Rock—"

She lifted a hand to his face and his voice disappeared. Why was it that something as simple as her touch made him feel whole?

"I'm okay," she said softly. "I trust you. Or at least I want to, but I need to know what's going on. I need the truth."

His instincts screamed at him to tell her everything. About her father, about himself. About how he was falling in love with her.

He stared into Blue's eyes, fighting an internal battle he had no idea how to win.

"I won't lie to you." He had nothing else to offer, except the one thing he wanted to and never could. Himself. He couldn't even protect her properly. He knew that now. He was way too involved personally.

He couldn't tell her the whole truth. But he could do his best to keep her alive.

He'd have himself pulled from the case first thing in the morning.

But he had to taste her one last time.

EIGHT

Diego lowered his mouth, giving her time to pull away, praying she wouldn't.

Her lips parted further and he sighed into her mouth as he covered hers with his own.

Her hand cupped his face, then slid slowly around his neck, her fingers weaving into his hair. She touched him like . . . a lover. Not a sex partner. A lover.

He'd never known there could be a difference.

He moved his mouth to the corner of hers, then trailed small, gentle kisses to her jaw. He'd never once in his life felt gentle.

"What are you doing to me, Blue?" he whispered against her smooth cheek.

She arched her neck, and his lips followed the sweet curve from her ear to the curve at the base.

"I don't know. Why do I want this?" she answered. "Why do I trust you?"

He lifted his head. "Because you can."

"I have been betrayed one too many times before, Diego."

"I know."

She lifted one brow in question.

"I was sent here to protect you. I know a lot about you."

She dropped her hand and began to struggle to get out from under him. "Move off of me," she demanded.

His sharp grunt when her knee connected with his taped thigh stopped her. "Blue—"

She was breathing rapidly, her dark eyes glittering. "I want up, now."

Diego knew he should back off, give them both some space. Instead he levered his bad thigh over hers, ignoring the pain, trapping her against the couch. "There are things we both want and can't have, Blue. Just like there are things I want to tell you and can't." He shook his head sharply when she opened her mouth to retort. "I want to. But I owe loyalty to others besides you. I gave my word to them first."

"Apparently you don't owe loyalty to anyone but yourself. Or your job. And I'm not referring to the one you have with me. By the way, you're fired."

"I do owe you loyalty, but you have no idea of the constraints I'm working within."

"Why? Why do you care what I think?" They were almost shouting now.

He pushed his face into hers, his voice lowering to

a raw whisper. "Because I have never cared about anything or anyone in my life. I do my job. That is the most I ever allow anyone to expect from me and it's the most I've ever expected from myself. And that has always been enough." He broke off, breathing unevenly. "Until now," he said hoarsely.

"What changed?"

"You." She shifted slightly under him, making him swallow hard. "You made me care."

"I didn't do anything. I don't need to be cared for."

He took her mouth in a hard kiss. She stiffened in surprise, but in seconds her mouth softened, her lips parted. He gentled the kiss, needing to feel it returned as much as to know he was capable of giving it.

Long seconds later he lifted his head. "Yes, you do," he said softly. "And so do I."

"You take care of you pretty well, Diego Santerra."

"Maybe I'm tired of that. Maybe for the first time I think it would be nice to share that load." Until he'd said the words, he hadn't realized the depth of truth in them. And the truth terrified him.

She didn't look at him; she looked into him. He fought against the urge to close down, to shut her out.

"What load are you carrying, Diego? Why hasn't anyone cared for you before?"

"There was no one at first anyway." The words came surprisingly easily, as if they'd been waiting all along for someone just to ask. "After a while it was easier not to let anyone. The only person I knew for certain I could rely on was me."

"No childhood," she recalled softly. "Why?"

"I was left on the doorstep of a mission in Arizona when I was four months old. There was a note saying 'feed him' signed with a big Z tucked in my blanket."

She stroked his face, her eyes sad, not with pity, but with compassion. How had he fooled himself into believing he didn't need compassion? He did need. Deeply.

"So unfair," Blue said. "At least she tried."

"The sisters have no idea who left me. I was naked, unwashed, dehydrated, and severely malnourished." He paused. Not once in his life had he repeated this story, not in this kind of detail. Not even to Del.

She continued to stroke his cheek, brushing the hair from his forehead and tracing his brow. It was soothing. Reassuring. There was no judgment here, never would be. Instead she offered peace. Understanding. Sanctuary.

His voice was a bit rougher as he continued. "Sister Marguerite, the one who found me, was a movie buff. Zorro was one of her favorites. The Z on the note caught her, I guess."

"Hence your name. Diego was Zorro's real name, right?"

"In *Mark of Zorro*, according to the sister."

"You never saw the movie?"

Her smile caught at his heart. He shook his head. "Santerra was the name of the manufacturer of the blanket I was wrapped in. Sister Marguerite said it was probably what saved me from the desert nights and was as much my guardian as anything."

Blue's smile was wistful. His breath caught in his throat.

"Quite a legacy. A lot of babies' names come out of a book bought for two ninety-five at the local supermart. Yours was chosen with love and affection just for you. Not a bad start."

He stared at her in wonder, feeling his eyes burn. "You are amazing."

"I'm not anything. I'm just me."

She had no idea the gift she'd just given him. "I've always defined myself by my past. By the fact that I came from nowhere, with nothing. How did you just change that?"

"Just lucky, I guess?"

"Do you have any idea how special you are?"

"Hardly special." Her smile faded, becoming wistful, then a bit sad. "You know who I am?" She released a long slow sigh. "I'm someone who has been running from her dreams all her life. I tried to become what I thought I should be and failed at that too. I learned a lot about myself when I divorced Anthony. I am strong." She looked into his eyes. "But being strong all the time is exhausting. I was tired of trying to figure out what everyone needed me to be. I was tired of trying to figure out what I needed me to be. Since then I have been hiding, playing it safe. If you don't dare, you don't risk failure."

"And you deprive yourself of the chance to savor sweet success."

"What do you know about success, Diego?" she asked sincerely. "When you do your job, complete your missions or whatever it is you call them, do you feel like you've done what you were put here to do? Does it satisfy you?" She looked away, then back at him. "I am happy, Diego. My life is a good one, full of friends and family who love me, whom I love in return. But I'm not satisfied." She released a sigh that came from somewhere deep inside her.

"Do you understand?" she asked plaintively.

He pressed his lips to hers in a soft, slow kiss. When he raised his head his eyes were burning. He felt fierce and tender all at the same time. "Yes, I do."

"Is it okay not to be satisfied? Do I risk the peace I've found on trying to do something I have no idea I can do? On reaching for a dream? What if I fail again? How do I pick up the pieces then?"

"Oh, Blue."

"Then I can't even say that I'm only doing this until I'm ready to try that. That will be gone. There won't be anything left to reach for."

Reach for me. He badly wanted to be the man she reached for. The goal she'd work for.

But what the hell did he have to offer her?

His whole life, his goals and values, were shifting in front of him like sand being blown across the desert.

"There are always new dreams." Was this really

him talking? She talked about risk. Did he dare? And what if he failed?

"Are you satisfied with your life, Diego?"

He shook his head, realizing the truth only in that exact moment. "I've never asked myself that before," he said honestly. "As a kid I spent most of my time feeling cheated out of a life. I had no idea that I was wasting the only one I had."

"You were never adopted?"

He shook his head. "No. It took a long time to get me healthy. I was a sickly, scrawny kid."

"You seem to have overcome that fairly well."

His mouth curved. "The sisters were determined. Their boss is almost as relentless as you are."

She smoothed her finger over his lips.

Don't ever stop touching me, Blue. I need to be touched. Often. Forever. The words lodged in his throat.

"Where did you go when you left there?"

"I left when I was seventeen. I guess it's a measure of how strong they were that they got me to stay that long. That I even lived to see seventeen."

"Docile and quiet kid, huh?"

"Not hardly."

"Did you finish school?"

"High school. I drifted all over the South. Ended up in Miami."

"Florida." She said the word as if she was testing the idea of it. "I don't see you as a beach bum."

Fear started to creep inside him. She was looking at him as if he was someone worth knowing. Worth caring about. Worth loving even? He didn't deserve this, didn't deserve her. *Don't risk this kind of pain*, his head screamed at him. His heart wasn't listening.

His smile faded. "Drug runner."

"Really?" Her interest was sincere, but there was no censure. "And you got out alive? Pretty scrappy."

Perversely her acceptance made him angry. It couldn't just be okay, could it? Diego purposely shoved reality like a hard wedge between them. "How do you know I got out? How do you know I'm not in with Jacounda on all this?"

Blue didn't even blink. "Why rescue me from him? Jacounda. The men who had me said that name. Is he the one testifying, the one who sent them after me? I've never heard of him. Why would he want me dead?" She looked up at him. "Will you tell me that? Don't you think I at least deserve that much?"

Diego sighed heavily and levered himself off of her and away from her touch. He felt cold, deep down cold.

She let him go. "I guess not, huh." It wasn't a question.

"You do deserve it, Blue. And a whole lot more." A whole lot more than me. "The best I can offer you is that when the trial is over and everyone is safe, I will do my best to have the information released to you." He looked at her. "It's not up to me. I wish it was, but it's not."

"But you do know." Blue shoved off the couch and paced the length of the cabin. She stopped, looked at him, then, with another sigh of disgust, resumed pacing.

Diego made himself watch her fight the internal battle, fight the frustration of not being in control, of being left out in the cold with no information to help her to deal with it all. If he were in her place, he would feel just the same. This was a mistake.

He'd told himself that if it had gone according to plan, this would never have been an issue. But he knew now he was fooling himself. As soon as he got to know Blue, he knew Del's insistence on keeping her in the dark was wrong. He also understood her father's need to protect his daughter. But at what cost? To both of them. And here she was, at risk anyway.

"I'll do my best, Blue. I'll start on it as soon as I get back in. I'll send word to John. Or come back myself."

She stopped midway across the room and turned to face him. "Come back? Where are you going?"

Diego couldn't deny the small burst of pleasure her reaction gave him. Just as he couldn't deny the equally strong surge of anger he felt at hearing that tiny thread of vulnerability and fear in her tone. Dammit, this wasn't right!

He pushed to a stand, grateful when she closed the distance between them.

"You're leaving me here with John?"

"He's good at his job, Blue. He'll take care of you."

"I don't want to be taken care of!" She moved closer to him, invading his personal space again, pushing the limits. "I don't want to be left here. What I want is for you to tell me what is going on so that I can decide for myself what I want. What I want is—" She broke off suddenly, and started to whirl away.

Diego snagged her arm with his good hand and pulled her back to face him. "What you want is what?" He was standing perfectly still and yet his heart was racing as if he were running uphill. He gentled his hold and his voice. "What do you want, Blue?"

She began to tremble. He felt the fine tremors under his fingertips. He stepped closer, wanting her in his arms yet knowing it had to be her choice.

She moved against him easily, a long sigh easing out of her throat as she slid her arms around him so as not to press against his sling.

He pressed her head to his chest, knowing she'd hear the pounding of his heart, wanting her to know how she affected him. She held him tighter, until he could feel her heartbeat. It matched his so closely that after another few moments he could feel only one.

He had no idea how long they stood like that. He had pulled her into his arms to comfort her, but the way she held him nourished some deep, unmet hunger inside him. He could have stood there with her for an eternity and still not been sated.

Long minutes later he slipped his hand up to her face. He smoothed the stray wisps of hair that had long ago escaped her braid and tucked them gently behind her ear. He let his fingers trail over her temple and cheekbone, along her jaw, before coming to rest on her chin. He nudged it up, tilting his head down as she raised her eyes to his.

"What is it you want, Blue?" he asked, his voice barely a rasp.

"You," she answered without hesitation. "I want you." She pressed a heartbreakingly gentle kiss on his lips then started to pull away.

"Come here." He pulled her back against him. "I want you, too, Blue."

She kissed him, her mouth melting into his until he swore he couldn't tell where he ended and she began. The pain in his shoulder and thigh receded as other parts of his body responded to her in a rage of need and want. He shifted his hips against her but nothing eased the ache.

"I need you, Diego," she whispered against his mouth. "Like I have never needed before." He cupped her face with his free hand, weaving his fingertips into her hair, deepening the kiss even as she did the same, until they were mating as fiercely with their mouths as he wanted to with his whole body.

Panting hard, they finally broke apart. He gripped her hair, holding her head gently but firmly close to his. His eyes searched hers. He knew his expression revealed the primal ferocity of what he was feeling. The need to claim was as strong as it was outrageous. He knew it and couldn't contain it, couldn't control it. Didn't want to. He wanted her to be his in some basic incontrovertible way.

"I have never wanted like this, Blue. Never felt the need to— The desire to have you is—" There were no words for this. Could she feel it too?

"Yes, Diego. Oh yes," she said. And he knew then

she did understand. It was like finding the other half of himself.

For the first time in his life he felt whole. Complete.

"What you do to me, Blue. What you do to me." He backed up, pulling her with him, until the couch bumped into his legs. He slid his arm out of the sling, ignoring the burning sting of pain.

"Diego—"

"Shhh. Come here, Blue." He let her go long enough to lever himself down onto the couch.

"But your thigh—"

"Straddle me. I want to feel you."

She moaned, her knees buckling slightly. "But—"

He reached up with his good hand and grabbed her hip. "Come here." He tugged her body to his, needing to feel her heartbeat against his.

She straddled his hips, careful to keep her weight off his legs, pressing down hard on the juncture of his legs, making them both groan as their bodies moved against one another automatically seeking relief. Then she came into his arms, laid her body against his as if she'd always belonged there. She fit into him as if their contours had been sculpted with the other specifically in mind.

"Yes," he sighed into her mouth as he felt the sweet pressure of her breasts cushion his chest, absorb the pounding of his heart.

She slipped her mouth from his, trailed soft warm kisses along his jaw to the tender skin below his ear. He felt healed. As if the scars on his soul were being smoothed over one by one with each touch of her mouth to his body.

"I have never felt like this, wanted like this, needed like this," she whispered into his ear. "Not ever. You make me feel . . ."

He nudged her head up and looked at her. "Whole."

She smiled. He loved her smile, bathed in the warmth of it.

"Yes," she said. "Exactly." She dropped a soul-healing kiss on his lips.

"With you I feel this need to . . ." She shook her head. "I can't even say it."

"Claim?"

"Yes," she said, her tone urgent. "And more than that. Diego, this is so unlike me. So unlike what I thought being strong was all about. And yet I feel a need to be claimed too." She touched his face. "By you."

She tightened her knees around his hips, pressing down on him even as his body lifted, looking for, needing that complete connection.

He brought her mouth to his and kissed her long and hard. "This is just the start of the way we will claim each other."

"Oh yes," she said. She kissed him this time, riding his hips hard until they were both on the brink.

"I want to feel you inside me, Diego."

He didn't answer. Couldn't answer. The need to drive deeply into her went far beyond physical satiation. And he knew her need came from that same intangible, unexplainable place. He reached between them and unsnapped his jeans. She slipped off of him and shimmied out of her jeans, then pulled off her shirt.

His jeans unzipped, his shirt unbuttoned, he stilled. "You're beautiful, Blue." He was staring at her. The fierce need, the want, the acceptance, the understanding, the love he found in her eyes brought him to his knees. He reached for her. She helped him slide his jeans to his thighs, careful of the tape, then pushed his shirt open so that when she straddled him they were skin to skin.

"You're so warm." She placed one hand on his cheek, the other on his chest at his heart. Her fingers trailed to the edge of the bandages peeking out from his open shirt. "Your shoulder—"

"No. I want you. Need you. That"—he nodded to his wounded arm—"is superficial." He gripped her hip with one hand, and held himself with the other, guiding himself into her. "You heal far deeper wounds with just a touch."

He looked to where their bodies were slowly joining. She looked down, too, and gasped as he began to penetrate her. "Yes," she sighed. As he slid all the way inside her their gazes lifted and locked on to each other. "Heal me," she said roughly. "Let me love you."

He surged upward, heedless of his injuries, of the pain lancing his body, feeling only the heat of her, gripping him, holding him deeply within her. He couldn't get close enough.

He pulled her up and buried his face in her chest, then turned his head and took one of her nipples softly into his mouth, suckling her.

Blue cupped his head and watched his mouth move on her. Her eyes burned at the erotic yet tender picture he made as he took from her. She gave willingly and received far more than she could have ever imagined in return. She gave all of herself to him, willingly.

Heat and need coiled inside her. His lips and tongue pulled and laved her nipple as he surged inside her over and over. She tightened around him, holding him inside her as tightly as she could. She kissed the top of his head, gasping as he caught her other nipple in his mouth.

He lifted his head, his mouth wet from loving her, and looked into her eyes. "You are mine, Blue Delgado. I give myself to you." He bucked beneath her and she felt him begin to climax.

She took his mouth and her climax exploded inside her as she gave herself to him completely.

Blue had no idea how long they held each other, how long she held him inside her body and her heart. They drifted into a long series of slow kisses, wandering caresses, and softly spoken words.

Diego rubbed her back with the palm of his hand. "John will be back soon. We should get dressed," he said against her neck.

"I know. Life intrudes." She nuzzled against his cheek. "I don't like life sometimes."

"Me either. I would stay right here forever."

Blue laughed softly. "Well, I think if I had a choice, I'd prefer a nice soft bed, you healthy and whole"—she picked at the scraggled mess her hair had become and rubbed at the dirt on her face—"me bathed."

He rubbed her cheek with the pad of his thumb. "You're beautiful."

He was so serious, it made her grin. But as she stared into his pale eyes she grew serious too. "So are you, Diego."

Now it was his turn to smile, though it was a dry one.

"Oh, how I love it when you do that," she said.

"What?" he asked.

"Smile."

"I like it too. Thank you for that, Blue." He pulled her to him for another long lazy kiss. When they both started to stir again, he pulled back with a groan. "We have to—"

"I know, I know. Hide me from crazed killers and plot ways to foil their nefarious schemes."

He grinned at that. "Woman after my own heart."

She kissed him hard. "Man who already has mine," she said quietly. Then carefully slid off of him, sighing as he eased from her body, but turning away before he could pull her back.

Feeling cold and oddly alone, she reached for her jeans.

"You have mine too," he said into the sudden quiet.

NINE

Before Blue could comment, she heard the slide of his zipper and the rustle of his shirt as he fumbled with the buttons. She finished pulling her shirt back on, then turned. "I'll do that." She brushed his hands aside and finished the task.

He pulled her head to his and kissed her deeply. "Thank you, Blue," he said against her lips.

Her eyes drifted shut as she whispered, "Please don't leave me here."

He ached with the knowledge of what that simple request had cost her. "I don't want to." He stole another soft kiss, then another. She opened her eyes when he stopped. "But your safety is most important. I'm too involved, Blue. I should have let John call in a replacement yesterday after I was shot. I can't protect you like this. Both my body and my mind aren't fully able."

She pulled back a little. "I'm not exactly helpless,

Diego. As you probably know, I made it three quarters of the way through the police academy in the top five in my class. I know when to shoot and when to duck. Don't protect me. Educate me so I can protect myself." She gave a meaningful glance to his sling. "So we can protect each other."

"I already have a partner."

"Is there a law that says you can only have one?"

"Is that why you want me to stay?"

"If all I wanted was a partner to help get me out of here, I could use John."

"You don't know John very well."

"Well enough to know I'd make him so miserable that he'd be relieved to let me take care of myself."

Diego almost smiled. "I'll be sure to tell him that."

"I'm sure he'll care."

"You have no idea how much. He's putting his life on the line for you too."

Blue looked away, her cheeks flushing. "I'm sorry. That was ungrateful of me." She looked back. "But it's not like I asked him to. He's not doing this for me. He's doing it for whoever asked him to. Who asked him, Diego? Who do you work for?"

"You never answered my question."

Disgusted, she tried to pull away from him. He held her tight.

"Will you answer mine if I answer yours?" she asked evenly.

"As best I can, yes."

"You mean as best as you will. You know the whole story, so you *can* tell me, but you won't."

"Are you going to answer me?"

A hint of a smile played at the corners of her mouth. "You are almost as bad as I am, Santerra. Like a bulldog sometimes."

"We make quite a pair, Blue Delgado."

She searched his face, looking inside him the way only she seemed able to do. "Yes, Diego Santerra. I'm beginning to think we do." She pressed one hand against his face, molding his cheek with her palm. "That's why I don't want you to go. I'm just finding out that maybe I want to risk dreaming again. Maybe you could be part of that dream. I don't know, but I want to find out. If you walk out that door, I'm afraid I'll never have that chance."

His soul connected to her words, to her wants, to her needs. They were his, too, yet his heart ached at her declaration. "I can't promise you anything, Blue. Hell, I can't even tell you what is going on here." He brought his hand up to frame her face as she had his. "So soft," he whispered, pressing his fingertips to her temple. "And yet so strong."

Blue stared at the man who had turned her world upside down in ways she hadn't thought possible. "You make me feel so protected, yet I know that you respect my strength, that you expect me to be myself and want me that way." She let her fingers trail over his lips. He kissed them, making her draw in a soft, sharp breath. "Do you know how incredible that is to me?" She replaced her fingers with her mouth, kissing him gently at first, then more firmly, until she was pouring every ounce of feeling she had into it. When she finally pulled away, they were both breathing heavily again. "So maybe it's time for you to dream a little too."

"I've never wanted to before. I don't know if I can now. I'm not sure I even know how."

His beautiful pale eyes were so bleak, she felt her eyes burn. "Then think of me—us—as a goal, as a mission to be accomplished."

"That's just it, I don't see how there can be an us. My job . . ." His voice trailed off and he looked away, shaking his head.

She turned his face back to hers. "I'm not asking you to give up anything. Yes, I want to know what is happening here, to me, and why. That's normal, I think. And yes, there is a part of me that understands why you can't tell me, as frustrating as that is. I respect your integrity even as I want you to trust me enough to tell me anyway." A small smile curved her lips. "See, I don't ask for much."

"Blue—"

"Shhh," she said, stopping his argument. "I don't know what I'm really asking for here. When you kissed me on Red Rock, you said no rules, no promises. I'm not asking for any now. All I want is what you can give me. A day, an hour. I want more, Diego, I won't lie. I might even want it all." She held his gaze squarely. "But I will take whatever I can get. I already know it's better than nothing at all."

"You don't know what you're saying. You don't—"

"Oh yes I do. You're just afraid I really mean it."

"You don't know me, don't know what I'm capable of doing, what I have done."

"Drug runner, secret-agent man, and cook," she shot back. "Anything else?"

He shook his head, but the look in his eyes made her shiver.

"That's right, Blue." She hated the emptiness in his voice. "Cold. That's what I am. I've been a drug runner and I can cook for myself. But you got my current job description wrong. You know what I am? I'm a killer, Blue. Uncle Sam's lethal weapon. They point me at the bad guys and I get rid of them. However I can, whatever it takes. I'm like a damn machine. And I'm damn good at it. Is that what you want?"

"Since when did Uncle Sam start recruiting teenage drug runners?"

Diego blew out a heavy sigh of disgust. "Aren't you listening to anything I'm saying?"

"Yes," she said calmly. "How did you go from working for the bad guys to working for the good ones?"

"It's not that black-and-white, Blue. They just offered me a better deal, one where I could do what I was already doing, but it was all legal. The only difference was if I got caught, I didn't do jail time, I got killed. And frankly I didn't really care about that. It's just a matter of time anyway."

"Diego—"

"No, Blue. Don't assign me values and morals I don't have. I'm no different from most of the men I take out." He shook his head. "Take out. I mean kill. I kill people, Blue."

"Can you live with yourself? Your decision to do this?" She lifted her hand to stop his response. "I already know the answer to that. Of course you can or you wouldn't do it. Couldn't do it." She shook her head when he opened his mouth to speak. "No, don't try to convince me otherwise. You are telling me that you are a stone-cold killer with the morals and mind of a criminal who just happens to work on the right side of the law. I know that to be wrong. I've witnessed firsthand your emotions, your morals, your mind." Her tone was urgent now. "I hate it that there is even a need for a job like yours. But I also know they were damn lucky to find you. No one who is as committed as you are is just 'doing his job.' This is you, Diego, and that's not a bad thing." She grabbed his arm when she saw emotion flicker in his eyes. "You're not a bad thing. Whoever hired you understood that. He didn't just give you a better job opportunity, he gave you your life. Don't you see that?" She relaxed her grip on his arm. "So the answer is yes, you are what I want."

"Blue, I—" He broke off and looked away.

She let him, knowing he was fighting a battle in which only he could decide the victor. Waiting was the hardest thing she'd ever done.

When he finally did look back at her she wanted to weep at the emotions filling his eyes. It was all the answer she needed. Her mouth was on his before he had a chance to speak.

He tugged her hard against his body, heedless of his sling. "Blue, Blue," he said against her mouth. "What are you doing to me?"

Loving you. The words rang clearly in her mind, and in her heart.

He lifted his head, his eyes still glassy, his voice hoarse. "You make me feel things I've never— Hell, you make me feel, period." He cupped her face with one hand. "I don't want to leave you."

Blue's heart sank. "But you are."

"I can't do my job." He cut off her reply with a shake of his head. "No, it's precisely because I care too much that I have to get a replacement up here. The team is a good one, Blue. Solid. I trust them with my life, and I trust them with yours." He heaved a sigh, then traced her bottom lip with his finger. "And you have to believe that is the most precious thing to me right now. I have to know I am doing what is best for you." He lifted his sling slightly. "Between my arm, my leg . . ." He grabbed her gaze and held it tightly. "And my heart . . . I'm not even close to one hundred percent. Let me do what I have to do. And I plan to do whatever I can to get the okay to tell you everything."

"I want to hear it from you."

"You will."

"Is that a promise, Diego Santerra?"

"It's as close to one as I can make, Blue. You should know the truth."

"What is it that is so dangerous for me to know? I haven't done anything to anyone, heard anything, seen anything." She focused on her frustration and her fear. It was the only way she was going to keep from falling apart when he walked away from her.

"I'll do my best, Blue."

She reined in her temper and tried to smile for him. "Well, that's no small promise," she said softly.

"It's late. You should try to get some sleep."

The idea of going into a strange room all alone and shutting the door suddenly terrified her. A part of her knew she was being silly, but a larger part of her simply refused to face her demons alone in the dark.

She didn't realize her grip on his shirtfront had tightened until he pried her fingers loose and brought her hand to his mouth. She was trembling but was helpless to stop it.

"I'm okay," she said, knowing she was anything but. She had no idea how long they'd been standing there, but his leg had to be beyond throbbing. And his shoulder couldn't be any better, as much as she'd been clinging to him. "You need your rest too."

"I'll be fine," he said.

"And we are both full of it."

His mouth curved slightly. "There is a lamp on the nightstand in there. Leave it on. If you need me, I'll be right out here."

She nodded, knowing if she spoke she'd be begging him to join her. Not for sex. She wanted him wrapped around her, knowing he'd keep her safe. And to know he'd be okay as long as he was in her arms. Sleeping apart didn't feel right.

She stepped out of his arms while she still could. "Which one?" She motioned toward the two doors.

"On the left."

When she reached the door, she turned back to him. "Will you be here in the morning?"

"Yes."

She didn't have to ask if he was still leaving, but at least this wasn't good-bye. Not yet anyway.

Just then the front door flew open, startling both of them. McShane filled the doorway, his entire body screaming tension.

"Word just came up the hill. They're on the way. Get her loaded and out of here. I'll slow them down as much as I can."

"Transport?" Diego asked, already limping across the room to the kitchen.

"Four-wheel-drive truck. One." John crossed to the front of the cabin. "That we know of anyway."

"How did they find us?" Blue asked, not moving. One second she was immersed in Diego, and the next, the world rudely interrupted again. She was having a harder time making the transition than Diego was.

They ignored her, or maybe they hadn't heard her at all. She supposed it made no difference. They continued to swap questions and information in terse abbreviated lingo. She understood about half of it. The most important part was crystal clear. Jacounda's men knew where she was and they were coming to get her.

Diego one-armed a long black duffel bag to John. "Put that in the Jeep, passenger side, zipper up."

"Done." John hefted another black multizippered bag and left the cabin.

Diego turned to Blue. "When we get in the Jeep, I want you in the back, on the floor. Don't lift so much as a hair on your head until I tell you to."

Blue just stared at him. The machine had surfaced. Diego the man was nowhere to be seen. Part of her ached for the loss. The other was fascinated by this side of him. The complex combination was downright irresistible.

John came back in, talking into a small microphone wired to his collar. "Out in less than two." He stopped in front of them. "Time to go. You've got about a five-minute lead. Track C seems the best bet in getting down. It's clear right now. Rico has been taken out of the checkpoint. No word on why. T.J. will meet you at Point B." He paused. "They'll take her from there."

A moment of silence passed as the two men stared at one another. Blue knew enough to deduce that Diego was being pulled from the case.

She wanted to speak up in his defense, make it clear that he had already chosen to do that, but she doubted he'd appreciate the interference. In fact, right now, that's how she felt. Like an interference in his whole life.

"Understood," Diego finally said, then looked to her. "Let's move."

"Your arm and your leg—" She broke off, not entirely sure what she meant to say to him. Something felt wrong, terribly wrong. It went beyond the threat of danger. He was too impersonal, when less than five minutes ago he had been anything but.

"I'll get you to the bottom of the mountain," he said.

John broke in. "I wouldn't send him if I—"

"It's not me I'm worried about!" She hadn't meant to shout, but it got their attention. The sudden silence was almost deafening.

John looked from her to Diego, then said, "Get gone. I'll try to buy you another five to ten."

Diego headed for the Jeep. Blue followed, turning to him just before climbing in the back. "I could drive. It makes more sense. They'd never think I'd be the driver. I'll wear a baseball hat or something."

"Nice try. Get in and hold on. The ride won't be a smooth one."

"Do you really think you're capable of defensive driving, if it comes to that?"

She hadn't meant to hurt him. Hadn't thought she could. But she hadn't mistaken that brief flicker of emotion before his expression closed her out completely. She put her hand on his good arm. "I didn't mean it that way, Diego. I want us both to get out of here safely. I just want to help."

"I'll get you to the checkpoint. You and T.J. can hash it out from there. Get in, Blue. We're wasting time."

She swallowed her impatience, but only as long as it took to get in the back and hunker down. As soon as Diego was in and they were moving, she spoke, raising her voice to be heard over the noise inside the doorless Jeep.

"So you plan to dump me on this T.J. person and that's it? Another of your illustrious team, I take it. Just how many of you guys are there?" She wasn't sure he would answer. Her body screamed in revolt as they bounced over the rutted road. She felt as if she'd been used for batting practice. When he finally spoke she heaved a sigh of relief. Something to focus on besides the pain. And the fear.

"We started with twelve. The Dirty Dozen. That was about ten years ago. There are six of us left and a team leader. He's the one testifying. Once he's done, he will, for all intents and purposes, cease to exist."

"Where will you go once we get to the checkpoint?" she asked.

"We have to get there first."

"*When* we do, what next?"

There was a pause, then he said, "I go back to headquarters and fight like hell to bring you in and brief you when this is all over."

She slipped her hand between the seats and touched his arm. He stilled for a second between shifting gears and she pressed her fingers tighter.

"Thank you, Diego."

"I think it's the right thing to do," he said almost dismissively. But he did nothing to stop her from touching him. His skin was warm, alive, reassuring. "If I succeed, I hope you agree."

That surprised her. "Of course I will. Why wouldn't I?"

He didn't answer. A split second later two bright beams of light popped over the ridge behind them, about a half mile back.

Out of habit, she started to lift her head to look.

"Get down as far as you can," he ordered. "Don't move unless I tell you to."

"Okay."

She saw him slip the sling off his left shoulder so he could use both hands. Until now he'd been using one hand to steer and shift at the same time. She had no idea how much damage the bullet had done to his shoulder, but she did know this was not going to help the healing process. She also knew she could argue over who should be driving until she was hoarse and it wouldn't change the current seating arrangements.

There was a pop and the Jeep made a sudden swerve to the right. Diego quickly pulled them back onto the road.

"What was that?" she yelled, unsure if she really wanted to know.

"It's okay, just stay down."

She didn't know whether to growl at the "Me Tarzan" command or smile at his attempt to reassure her. Diego Santerra was easily the most complex man she'd ever known, except perhaps for her father. And she'd hardly had a chance to know him before he was taken from her life all together. She vowed right then and there, in the middle of a high-speed chase with what she suspected were bullets flying, that if they both got out of this in one piece, she would do everything she could to make sure she didn't lose this man from her life.

Another series of popping sounds rattled the air, followed by a thud and a sharp ping. Something had hit the Jeep. Or vice versa. Or both.

"Hold on," he yelled.

Blue pushed her feet against the passenger seat and grabbed onto seat-belt straps as the Jeep went careening off the dirt track. She cracked her head as the Jeep hit a bump. She grunted involuntarily, then swore.

She barely had time to get her vision clear when they bounced hard again, then again.

"You okay?" he called out.

She couldn't even answer, the jarring ride taking her breath away.

"Blue, answer me!"

"Fine," she managed, as loud as she could. The Jeep swerved to the left, sending her to the floor. She bit down hard on her lip to keep from screaming, not wanting to distract him any further. She heard the scraping of brush and the thwack of tree limbs as they beat against the Jeep. It felt as if they were hurtling straight down the mountainside. She didn't try to get back onto the seat. At this point she was numb anyway.

White beams of light darted in and out of the Jeep's interior like some sort of warped strobe light. If they were taking the direct route straight down, then so were the men following them. How had they been found so quickly?

She spared a thought for John. The delay he'd promised hadn't happened. Was he okay?

Blue purposely shut down that train of thought. She couldn't do anything about it at the moment and it would only cloud her mind with panic. And it was close to choking her already.

A huge bang rocked the Jeep almost onto its side, wrenching a scream from her that was totally beyond her control. Then her world went sideways.

She was thrown onto the seat as the Jeep careened wildly downhill on two wheels. After what felt like an eternity the worst happened. It rolled. After that she had no idea what was up or down. "Diego!" she yelled, but the word came out as a strangled gurgle.

It was like being in a clothes dryer, she thought abstractedly, wondering how much it was going to hurt to die like this. Everything was so fast and loud, she couldn't make sense of it all.

Then with a bang and a body-breaking lurch, they stopped. The sudden cessation of sound was the only way she understood just how deafening the crash had been. Dazed, she didn't try to move.

Alive. That was her first thought. She opened her eyes. It took her a second to realize she was staring out the rear window. She thought they were upside down, but she couldn't be sure. She couldn't see any headlights behind them. Guess rolling down the mountain was where they drew the line in deadly pursuit. A rough laugh forced its way out of her throat. She clamped down on it, afraid she would go straight into hysterics.

"You okay?"

Diego! His voice was rough, weak. Was he hurt? Or could she barely hear?

Calm down, Blue. She tried to breathe in and out slowly to clear her head. It was tough in her current position.

"Don't move," he ordered.

Did he sound stronger this time? Was she getting stronger? "I . . . don't think I can."

"You're hurt?"

She couldn't lift or turn her head without moving her whole body, she was tucked too tightly against the roof. "I'm not sure. Where are you? You okay?"

"I'm okay. We're upside down, wedged between two trees. Can you feel your toes? Your fingers?"

Uh-oh. Was she that bad? She swallowed the panic. It tasted horribly like blood. *Concentrate, Blue.* Her fingers were curled under her chin. She moved them. "Yes, fingers are okay." She heard the relief in her voice and tried to stay calm. Toes. They were wedged under her almost Indian fashion, but she could feel them. "Toes are okay."

"Neck, head?"

Control of her body returned slowly but steadily. "Other than being wedged in here like a sardine, okay, I think." She still tasted blood. She gingerly explored with her tongue, then her fingertips. "I think I cut the inside of my lip on my teeth. It's okay, though."

There was no answer. Her hard-won calm teetered dangerously. "Diego?"

It was a moment before he answered.

"Yeah."

"You aren't okay, are you?"

"I'm fine. I'm just . . . pinned."

Blue carefully straightened one leg as far as she could, then used her arms as leverage to uncurl her other one. She ached in some areas and hurt like hell in others, but she didn't think anything was cracked or broken.

"You shouldn't move. You could have fractured something."

"I think I'm okay. Just banged up a bit. You need me."

There was a long pause while she slowly worked her way around so she could see him.

"Yeah, I guess I do."

"Don't try to sound thrilled on my account," she shot back, using sarcasm to keep fear from taking over. How was she going to help him? What if she couldn't? What if he was really hurt? She pulled herself to the front. He was upside down, still strapped into his seat. The roof had caved in enough so that his head was resting on it. "Oh, Diego."

He tried to turn to look at her, but the angle they were at prevented it.

"Don't move, your neck might be—" She couldn't even say it.

"Trust me, I can feel all my extremities."

She breathed a sigh of relief. "If I unhook you can you slide out? I can put something under you to cushion your shoulder."

"It's not just the belt. My foot is wedged up under the dash. I can't move without doing some serious damage down there. My thigh is pinned under the steering wheel."

"Your good one or your bad one?"

"I think they both qualify as bad at the moment."

Without thinking, she reached up and stroked the side of his face and neck. She needed to give comfort, and was instantly amazed that just feeling his skin, warm and alive against hers, brought her comfort too.

He groaned. She yanked her hand away. "I'm sorry, did that hurt?"

"No," he said, the word more a heartfelt sigh. "Don't stop touching me, Blue."

She immediately pressed her palm to his cheek. "We have to get you out of here. Tell me what to do to help you and I will."

Diego's face glowed oddly yellow in the dim light from the dashboard. The battery was still operational, but the headlights had apparently been smashed.

"It will take Jacounda's men quite some time to make it down into this ravine," he said. "There is no path near here. And even with night-vision equipment, the terrain is almost impossible to traverse on foot."

"I'm not worried about Jacounda."

"Well, you should be. If I didn't know my own men so well, I'd think he had someone on the inside. There is no way he should have found the cabin. Certainly not within the hour."

"Could they have followed John?"

"No." His response was instant and certain.

Blue hesitated, then said, "Do you think he's okay? They made up the time from the cabin pretty fast."

"I don't know." Blue knew the brutal answer was to protect himself as much as anything. She didn't push the subject.

"Is there any way to contact T.J.? Or signal the checkpoint?"

Diego sighed. "You do think like a cop, Blue. But no, not directly anyway. Too risky. They know too much. I don't know how, but they do."

"So what do we do? Wait for them to find us? There has to be a way to contact someone to get you out of here. You can't stay trapped in here."

"You should be worried about getting yourself out of here."

"That's it! Do you know where we are? Tell me where to go. I know these mountains fairly well. Well enough to get where I am supposed to be."

"No. You are not going out there alone."

"Well, I don't see what other choice we have."

Diego closed his eyes and swore under his breath. He was not sending her out there alone. Jacounda's latest team was good. Too good. If they got ahold of her after being thwarted so many times . . . No, he couldn't even consider it.

"Help get me out of here," he said. "I can take it from there."

"You just got done telling me you couldn't handle this when you left the cabin, now you—"

"Blue." His tone was both plea and command. "I can't let you go out there alone. I can't. Get me out of here. If my gear is still anywhere around here, I can—we can—set something up to buy more time."

"Your foot is pinned. And your thigh. What if you have internal bleeding? Diego, I can't take care of that. Of you. And I don't care what you say, I know you must be in considerable pain. There has to be a way to alert your team."

"There is one way."

"Good. Now we're getting somewhere. How? Just tell me and I'll do it."

"Blow up the Jeep."

TEN

Blue froze. "What?"

"The explosion will make Jacounda's men think we didn't survive the roll down the mountain. It will also alert the base checkpoint that we are in trouble and give them our location."

"You seem to have overlooked one minor detail. You are still in the Jeep." She looked at the smashed-in side panels and the trees and underbrush blocking the doorless sides. "For that matter, so am I."

"The back window can be taken out. The hard top should keep the structure, what's left of it, together."

"It's mostly smashed out anyway."

"Kick out the rest with the soles of your shoes. Put something over the edges then slide out."

Blue did as he said. It took some doing, but a few minutes later she managed to get through the jagged opening.

"I'm out."

He listened to her progress as she climbed around to the side of the Jeep. "I'm here," she said, less than a foot away to his left. He couldn't turn his head to look at her.

"The tree is blocking almost the entire door. The Jeep is wedged in pretty tight."

"My left arm is pinned against my side. I can't reach the seat lever," he said. "If you can slide your hand up and release it . . . I think that may do it."

"What about your foot? If the seat moves, you could be injured worse or—" She broke off, the mental image too strong.

"I can wiggle my toes, move my shoe slightly. I think it's just smashed in there too tight. If I can get my thighs loose, I can maneuver it out. The seat doesn't go back far enough to pull that hard on my foot."

"Okay." Blue held her breath and snaked her hand in the small opening between the tree and the Jeep frame. She found the lever, but releasing it was awkward from this angle. "Ready?"

Diego gripped the steering wheel with his free hand and ducked his head as best he could. "Yeah. Do it."

She pulled. Diego winced as the seat slid back, freeing his legs. The returned blood flow was intensely uncomfortable. Okay, it hurt like hell. But he was more focused on his foot. It was still stuck.

"Blue, come back in here. I need help."

She crawled back in to his side. His head was more

free now, having moved back to a more open, less caved-in area of the roof.

He looked at her. "My foot is still wedged in pretty tight."

"Okay, what do you want me to do?"

"Are either of my black bags still in here? I had them strapped in, but—"

Blue looked around the almost pitch-black interior and spied the two dark heaps almost immediately. "In the back, on the roof. They cushioned me, I guess, since they are underneath where I landed."

"There is a thin stick light in a tube pocket on the side of the smaller bag. Get that, then open the top-end zipper and get out the black leather zippered case."

Diego's voice sounded strained and she knew the pain was starting to go beyond endurance. Without another word, Blue followed his instructions, then brought them both back to the front.

"Open the case."

Holding the flashlight under her chin, she slid the zipper around and unfolded the case, revealing over a half-dozen knives. She looked up at him, accusation clear in her eyes. "It was you."

Diego didn't pretend to misunderstand. Too much had passed between them. At least in this he could offer her the whole truth. It wasn't nearly enough. "Yes, I stopped Leroy."

"You mean you stabbed him. You could have killed him!"

"No. I didn't aim to kill."

"He was trying to warn me. Why stop him?"

That she hadn't immediately turned suspicious and wary surprised him. He didn't feel deserving of her trust. But he couldn't ignore the pleasure he felt in knowing she truly believed in him. "We were already in place, watching you. Protecting you. You were never supposed to know we were there."

"But you were already working for me. Leroy had already—" He saw the light come on.

"Yes, we were responsible for him leaving. I'm not sure how he found out anything or how he managed to slip out and come back, but—"

"Why did you come to work for me?" she interrupted.

"We had word Jacounda had found you. I had to get closer."

"And Leroy's warning made it harder because then I knew something was wrong."

"I would have just maintained surveillance until the trial was over. Then I would have disappeared and you'd never have known I existed or that there had been a threat."

He didn't miss the flash of pain that crossed her face. It was in her voice when she spoke. "I don't want anyone hurt because of me or this. Whatever this is. But I'm not sorry that you came into my life."

"I don't want you in danger, Blue, but I feel the same way. You have had an incredible impact on my life. Whatever happens, I won't forget that. Or you. Ever."

"That sounds like good-bye."

Diego stared at her. He hurt like hell. His whole body throbbed and his head felt like someone had used it for target practice. There were a hundred things he wanted to tell her, but this was hardly the time or place.

"Let's get out of this thing, okay?"

"Yeah," she said softly, setting the case aside.

"Slide in between me and the steering wheel and reach down there to see what is trapping my foot."

She was already moving before he'd finished.

"Be careful. I don't know what might have broken off. There could be some jagged edges."

She aimed the penlight at the dashboard, fully aware of Diego's chest at her back and his thighs pressed against her head. She tried as best she could to avoid pressing against his bandaged thigh. If he was in pain, though, he was being very stoic about it.

"The gas pedal is bent sideways over your right foot. The dash is crushed down on top of that, trapping you left foot."

"Can you lift the pedal?"

"It would squeeze your other foot, but—"

"Do it."

She didn't argue this time. She didn't know if it was latent claustrophobia, fear of Jacounda's men, or just plain shock, but she suddenly *had* to get out of there. Had to get both of them out of there.

She pulled.

With a loud groan that belied how much pain he was in, Diego managed to drag one foot free. As soon as that space opened up, the whole dash started to cave in.

"Diego! Pull your other foot out now!" Blue grabbed his jean leg. Between the two of them they slid his toes free just as the edge of the dash came down onto the pedals. His legs were pulled up, pinning her under his knees. She wiggled out, rolled over, and looked at him.

"You okay?"

He was grimacing, but managed a tight nod. "Get the knife," he said between clenched teeth. "I need you to cut the seat belt. The latch is crushed."

Her hands were shaking as she slid the slim stiletto blade out of its sheath.

"It's like a razor, be careful."

"Gee, thanks," she muttered as she reached for an area of the chest strap that wasn't digging into his skin.

"When you cut it, get out of the way. I might fall on top of you." He shifted a little and groaned again. "Be sure to put the blade point down too."

Blue smiled despite her screaming nerves. "Now who's giving orders? I thought I was the boss here."

"You fired me, remember?"

Her nerves were strung too tight to keep up the pretense of banter. "You ready?"

She could see his strain in the way his jaw tightened. "Do it."

As carefully as she could, she slipped the blade under the strap, then pulled down, yanking her arm away as fast as possible. Diego lost his grip and came down hard on top of her.

He immediately tried to roll off of her, but his position, bad shoulder and thigh made it almost impossible.

"Blue?"

"It's okay," she said, her voice muffled. "The knife is out of the way."

She flipped her wrist as good as she could, sending the knife toward the back of the Jeep. It took several minutes of grunting and muffled curses, but they finally managed to untangle themselves. With very little talk, they worked to get themselves out of the Jeep. Once Diego had managed to drag himself clear, Blue went back in for his bags.

Diego had the penlight and, from his seated position, was scoping the immediate area for a clear spot. He eventually found one about a hundred feet away. He half crawled, half dragged himself over there. His shoulder was a mess, the sling long gone. His thigh throbbed but was otherwise okay. His left foot was sore and badly bruised, but it was his right foot and ankle that kept him on the ground. He'd definitely broken some bones and twisted up his ankle to the point that standing upright wasn't going to happen anytime soon.

Blue made her way over to him. "Are you okay?" She dropped the last of his gear next to him. "What about your feet?"

"I'll live."

Even in the dark he could see her roll her eyes.

"Men. We have to get you out of here. How far from the Jeep do we need to be to blow it up? Just tell me how to do it."

Diego shook his head. "I'd say you were just in shock, but you really are something else, Blue Delgado." It was on the tip of his tongue to say her father would be proud to know she had his instincts and strong center.

She turned her attention from the Jeep to him. "I will probably go into a coma as soon as this is all over. It just seems like a waste of time to get hysterical now."

He had no idea where the laughter came from, but it felt good. Too good to stop.

She looked at him, but her mouth twitched and then she was sitting next to him laughing. He knew it was a release of the fear and tension of the last couple of hours as well as a diversion from the pain he was in, but it felt good.

"You don't laugh much, do you, Diego?" she said as their laughter finally died away.

That sobered him. "Never had much cause to."

"I'm not sure, but I think there is a compliment in there somewhere."

Their eyes met and she placed her palm against his chest. He caught her hand, covering it with his own, and pressed harder.

After a long moment he moved his hand away and she stood. "Tell me what to do."

He didn't say anything for a moment, then cleared his throat. "We have to move farther away. Find another rock or boulder to get behind for protection. I'll take care of the blast."

Blue groped around and found the penlight. "I'll see what I can find."

He was already sliding his gear closer to his hip. "Be careful, the ground is very uneven."

She smiled in the darkness. "I've spent a lot of time climbing around these hills. I'll be okay." She almost laughed at the irony. She'd just spent the last couple of hours charting completely unknown territory. She'd never felt less sure of herself.

It took surprisingly little time to get everything set up. Still, Blue knew it had to be getting close to dawn.

"Hasn't it been too long since we wrecked?" she asked as she crouched behind the boulder next to him. "For the explosion, I mean? Won't Jacounda's men know we had time to get out?"

It had taken them some time getting him away from the Jeep. Even though his injuries were far from life-threatening, Blue knew he was in pretty bad shape. She was amazed he'd held up as well as he had. Her cheeks heated. His stamina, especially considering their brief but passionate encounter earlier in the cabin, had to be almost depleted.

"That is a chance we have to take. It's a miracle we survived in the first place. The explosion will still make them wonder. Our best chance is to alert T.J. and the rest of the team." He shifted a bit, making more room for her. "Get down and cover your ears."

She did. Seconds later a huge explosion rocked the night, vibrating the ground and showering the entire area with debris. They'd discussed the possibility of starting a forest fire with the blast, but a quick survey of the area showed they were on a mostly rocky slope. The trees that had stopped their descent were part of a very small, solitary stand. If they burned, which they probably would, the fire would likely go no farther. Diego said the beacon would help them too.

When the smoke cleared and debris stopped raining down on them, they both lifted their heads and watched the Jeep, or what was left of it, burn.

"How long do you think it will take for your guys to show?"

"Under an hour if we're lucky."

Neither of them had to ask what would happen if they weren't.

Blue turned away from the burning wreckage and looked at Diego. Highlighted by the flames, his face was more austere and remote than ever. Her hand was on his cheek before she'd even realized her need to connect with him.

He immediately turned his cheek into her hand, the movement so instinctive, it made her throat ache.

"Diego," she whispered. *I don't want to walk away from you.*

He looked her directly into the eyes, as if he'd heard her thoughts. She started to pull her hand away, but he caught it and pressed it to his cheek.

"I've never known what it was like to be touched. Not like this."

She was stunned by the stark honesty in his voice,

the immensity of need she heard in his quietly spoken admission.

"I do need you, Blue."

"I'm right here."

He shook his head. "No, really need. When they popped us and I lost control of the Jeep, I—" He broke off on a harsh breath and swore.

"It's okay, Diego. We'll be okay."

"No!" he said with surprising vehemence. "No, it's not okay. You might have been killed. It's a miracle that neither of us was badly hurt. You were right. I shouldn't have been behind the wheel. My reflexes—"

"Shh, stop that," she ordered. "You were right. There was no other way. I would have most likely lost control of the Jeep the first time we were hit. At best I would have at least gotten a flat tire." He didn't say anything. "That was a joke."

"I thought you might be dead, Blue. It scared me. The thought of losing you terrifies me."

"Oh, Diego." She traced trembling fingers across his lips. He kissed them gently.

"I've never been scared before. I always figured the worst that could happen was that I'd die. And death didn't bother me."

"Diego, I—"

"It bothers me now. And that terrifies me too. I have no idea how to handle this, Blue. I don't want to be robbed of any chance I have to know you."

"Then I guess we'd better find a way to get us both out of here."

"It's not that simple."

"Nothing worth having is."

"But—"

"But nothing." She cupped his face. "I feel the same way. I don't want to miss out on the opportunity of knowing you either."

"Blue—"

"There has only been one other man in my life I have ever truly cared for. And I swore I would never put myself in the position of being that open and vulnerable again."

"Anthony?"

"Hardly," she said. "No, he was a mistake all the way around. Not only did I not choose wisely, but I was with him for all the wrong reasons. I was trying to do what I thought I should do. For my family. For me."

"Is that why you gave up the academy?"

"Yes."

"You still want to be a cop?"

She stroked his face. He'd been holding his bad shoulder with his free hand, but he let it go to touch her hair and neck.

Blue felt the connection between them like an electrical current making a full circuit.

"You'd make a good one, Blue. You have the instincts."

A soft smile curved her mouth. "It's in my blood. My father was in law enforcement. Of a kind anyway." She looked him directly in the eyes. "He was a man like you. A man whose principles wouldn't let him compromise. He gave up his family to keep us safe.

And when that didn't work, he ended up giving his life."

"I'm not sure I'm worth that honor, Blue. But thank you."

"That's who I meant. He's the other man. My mom closed off a part of herself when they divorced. She loved me, but we never . . . connected. But my father . . . I was fifteen when he came back to us. He was everything to me. I loved him, idolized him. I gave him everything I had to give. When they died . . . when he was truly gone—" She broke off and looked away for a moment. "I lost a connection I never thought I'd feel again. You can't describe it, but I feel that with you, Diego."

"That's the difference between us, Blue. I've never known what connection feels like. It was never a part of my life growing up. And when it could have been, later, as an adult, I didn't dare even try. I don't think I'd have known how anyway."

"Do you still feel that way?"

He brushed his fingers over her cheek. "No. You . . . understand me. You don't look at me. You look into me."

"And I like what I see, Diego. You should be proud of the man you've become."

"I want to be worthy of that, Blue. I don't know if I can be."

"What do *you* want, Diego? Is your life enough for you now?"

"I'm not sure anymore. I've never really let myself

want more than I've got. I'm not sure I'm ready to now. Are you?"

"I don't know what I want either, Diego," she answered honestly. "I do know that what I've settled for in the past is not enough." She turned her head and pressed her lips against his forearm, feeling his pulse against her mouth. Then she lifted her head and looked at him. "I do know I want you."

"Oh, Blue. I want you too." He pulled her toward him. "Come here."

She kissed him.

He gentled it when she would have pushed harder. "Your lip," he said.

"Kiss me, Diego."

He did. And it was the most profound moment of her life. To be wanted and to want in equal measure.

"Yes, Blue, I do want you," Diego said against her mouth as he released her.

She reached her hand up to his face, stopping just short of touching him.

"Don't stop," he said, his voice rough with both pain and need. "Touch me, Blue." *Heal me.*

He felt the pressure of her palm on his face and neck all the way to the core of his soul. A deep sigh welled up inside him and eased out on a long slow breath. He leaned back against the rock, cradling his bad arm, his legs relaxed, his ankle propped against one of his gear bags. His entire body was throbbing, and his head pounded as if he had a jackhammer for a pulse. And he didn't care. "How is it your touch makes everything else disappear?" he said, not even realizing he'd spoken aloud until she moved.

She rolled onto her knees, positioning herself between his thighs. She cupped his face, looking past any barriers he might have raised. He no longer tried. He didn't want to, not with her. Never with her.

"The same reason that I trust you without knowing exactly why. You understand me like no one ever has."

Before Diego could respond, all hell broke loose.

ELEVEN

Blue scrambled away from Diego and they both peered over the boulder.

Four men had entered the area between them and the Jeep, sending a stream of rock debris tumbling as they slid down the steep terrain.

Diego whipped up his hand so fast, Blue didn't see the lethal black blade he held poised between his fingers until it was eye level.

Her fingers gripped his good shoulder, but the wicked curving edge of the blade didn't move so much as a hair.

"Your guys?" She already knew the answer.

"No."

In the next instant he pressed a .40-caliber Glock into her hand.

"Can you shoot this?"

"Yes," she answered, automatically flipping the safety and checking the clip.

Before she could get her next question out, the scene in front of them distracted her. There was a pop, then one of the men stumbled, grabbing his chest as he fell to the ground less than fifty feet from their hiding place. Even in the dark Blue saw the dark pool spreading out beneath him.

The other three men immediately dove for cover or assumed defensive positions. Guns were suddenly in their hands, and an instant later bullets flew fast and furious.

Blue felt Diego's attention shift and she followed his gaze. A dark shadow emerged from the shadowed downslope to their right, but movement from one of the men in front of her snagged at her peripheral vision. She turned just in time to see the man sight down on Diego. Blue didn't think. She just took aim and fired. The man's gun went flying from his hand, which he was now grasping, obviously in pain.

Diego looked at her, and in that split instant she'd never felt so deeply connected to another human being. No words were spoken. None needed to be. They were a team in every way possible, in ways she'd never known existed.

Their attention returned immediately to their attackers. Blue's shot hadn't taken the man out, but the remaining two men had retreated into the shadows. She knew she'd blown their location, but no more bullets were fired.

"How many of your guys are out there?"

"Don't know." His voice was right in her ear.

"Well, the odds are in our favor."

"I don't know how many more are on the upside of the hill either." Diego shifted closer to her, tucking himself farther behind the rock. "Cover my back."

"What are you going to do? Don't you—"

"It's still over an hour till full light. I want you out of here before then."

She opened her mouth to argue, but a small rock clicked off the boulder in front of her. She braced her back against the rock and leveled the gun with both hands in one smooth move.

"Don't shoot, I'm the good guy."

McShane. Too much adrenaline combined with an overwhelming rush of relief made her snap, "You were almost a good dead guy."

John slid in behind Blue and Diego so silently, Blue wondered if he wasn't a ghost after all.

He spoke to Diego. "You okay?"

"About seventy-five percent."

"You toasted Del's Jeep." He smiled, looking at Blue, then back at Diego. "Guess he won't mind."

"What happened?" Diego asked.

John sobered. "The cabin is toast too."

Blue swallowed hard, but Diego just said, "You okay?"

"One hundred percent. I always was faster than you."

"What do we do now?" she asked.

John looked at her. "We take a little trip. You're going to Florida."

Diego's sharp, "What?" made her flinch.

John turned to him. "Orders came down just before I had to close up shop. Scottie and T.J. are out there. Two o'clock and four o'clock, following Code C. Downslope is clear."

"I want her out before daylight," Diego said.

"That's the plan. I called in for special transport for you."

"No. I'll make it out of here on my own."

John didn't argue the point.

There was a brief silence, then Diego asked, "What's the deal with Rico?"

John glanced at Blue, then back to Diego. "I guess she'll know all of this soon enough. He's back in Miami, being interrogated."

Diego swore under his breath. "Why?"

Blue could only imagine the trust his teammates must require in order to do their job. "How could he do that?" she demanded, her temper sorely tried. "How could he put his own men out there—"

"It's more complicated than you think." John paused, then sighed. "We found out he met a woman on a mission about twenty months ago. She got pregnant. He's been supporting her and the child."

"Jacounda found out about the child," Diego said.

John nodded at the same time Blue gasped. "Are they okay?"

McShane nodded again. "We've got her and their son in protective custody." He and Diego looked at each other for a long silent moment, then John moved back on his haunches. "It will all get squared away later." He turned to Blue, the subject obviously closed. "Same as before, you stay behind me, stop when I stop, move when I move. Do what I say when I say it. Let's go." He turned to Diego. "See you in Miami."

"Wait a minute, you can't just leave—" Blue's protest was cut off by Diego's hand on her arm.

"I have to finish here."

"You aren't in any shape to—"

"Go with him." She would have continued to argue, but the look in his eyes stopped her. She felt John retreat into the shadows behind her, but she didn't look away from Diego.

His voice dropped so only she could hear him. "It's important, Blue. More than you know." He loosened his grip on her arm, caressing the spot gently before letting her go. "Just remember, I wanted to tell you."

She felt suddenly cold and fought a shiver. "Tell me what?"

He just shook his head. "You're an incredible woman, Blue. I've never met anyone like you."

"Diego, I—"

"Will you make me one promise?"

"What?"

"Do what is in your heart. It's not too late, Blue. It's never too late. You're the one who taught me that."

A deep ache took hold of her heart and began to squeeze. "Will I see you again?"

He never got the chance to answer. The area between them and the Jeep exploded into sudden action.

"This is the diversion," John said tersely. "Let's move."

Diego had already turned away, tensed and alert to the renewed battle at hand.

She saw his blade hand come up. One instant the wicked black dagger was in his hand, the next instant his hand was empty.

McShane pulled her arm. "Now!"

She whispered, "I love you, Diego Santerra," but knew he hadn't heard her. Less than ten yards down the scrabbled slope, she stopped and yanked once on John's arm.

He turned back to face her, frustration screaming from every tendon in his face and neck. "What?"

"Why Miami?" He started to drag her with him, but she yanked again. "Tell me or I walk as soon as I'm off this mountain. And to hell with your secret mission."

"The trial is in Miami."

"I figured that. Who wants me there?"

He swore under his breath. "I'll fry for this."

"Tell me, John."

He looked her hard in the eyes. "Your father. He's testifying tomorrow afternoon against Hermes Jacounda."

Blue paced the small, well-appointed sitting room, stopping for the umpteenth time in front of the picture window. The hotel was beachside. She looked from the water to the body-packed sand. Miami was a hot sweltering place teeming with way too many people. Only one held her interest. And he was late.

About thirteen years late.

She'd begged information from John and everyone else that she'd come into contact with to no avail. She'd been in this room for almost twenty-four hours. It felt like an eternity. She listened to reports on the television about the trial. It had not been televised, but coverage outside the courtroom was virtually nonstop. Reports that Steve Delaney had testified earlier that day, giving documented proof of Jacounda's involvement in organized crime, had local journalists in a frenzy. No mention of Seve Delgado, the secret government team he'd been in charge of for over ten years, or Blue's existence was ever made.

It was as if it all had never happened. Was she supposed to pretend that too? Would her father duck out on her? "Protect" her yet again by disappearing. And who was he? Seve Delgado, leader of the renegade Delgado's Dirty Dozen? Or Steve Delaney, Miami detective, who'd worked undercover in Jacounda's organization for the last two years?

Blue fingered the blinds on the window, turning them one way then the other, before retreating to the couch. She sat with a sigh, but was almost immediately up on her feet pacing again. She wondered how many names her father had used other than his own in thirteen years. It was a meaningless concern, but her brain was on overload and focusing on the inane was the only thing keeping her from losing it altogether.

Her thoughts turned to Diego, as they had over

and over during the last twenty-four hours. It had been natural, as if she sought peace in just the thought of him. Instead she'd only found more turmoil. How was he? What was he doing? Was he already on another mission? He must know she was going to be told everything. Did that mean he wouldn't contact her again? After all, his job involving her was over.

She'd demanded to know the outcome of the episode on the mountain and had been assured that Agent Santerra was fine. She'd asked to speak to him but had been told he was not available. Swearing and threatening got her nowhere either.

She hated not being in control. The only demand she'd been granted was her insistence on talking directly to Tejo. He had been understandably concerned and very relieved to hear firsthand that she was okay. When she asked him if he'd been told everything, including why she was in Miami, he'd remained silent too long.

"You knew, didn't you?" she'd asked him quietly. "How could you not tell me, Tejo?"

"I didn't know," he said, and she believed him.

"But you're not surprised, not really."

Another pause. "No," he'd responded, the word a rough emotional whisper. "I always had this sense, this feeling. . . ."

His words had drifted off, her uncle obviously too overcome to continue.

"I understand, Tejo," she'd said, her own throat thick with tears. "You couldn't give me false hope."

"Or myself," he'd said.

"Are you coming to Florida?"

"I don't know. I will make that decision later, after you've talked to him." When she protested, he said, "Do what you need to do, Blue. I'll take care of myself."

Blue heard Diego's last request in her uncle's words. *Do what is in your heart.* She paced back to the window, thinking over everything that had happened. In the past several days. In the past several years.

What was she going to do now?

Just then the door to the hallway opened and one of the guards that had been posted there since her arrival poked his head in. "Miss Delgado?"

She turned, her heart pounding. "Yes?"

"Your father is here."

Diego swiveled his chair away from the window. Watching the snow cover the distant slopes of the Rockies from his perch on the twentieth floor of the Denver office building only brought his thoughts back to the one person he'd spent the last three months trying to forget.

He looked at the man sitting opposite the large walnut desk. This would be the last time he saw his boss. At least the last time he would look at him and know he was looking at Seve Delgado. Del's transformation into his new life would include plastic surgery and a number of other alterations. Understandably, no one was to know where this was taking place, or where he would go or who he planned to become once he was healed. Not even his daughter.

"You're still not prepared to give me an answer?" the older man asked.

"When do you leave?"

One thing about Del hadn't changed. If he was frustrated with Diego's continued stubbornness, which Diego knew he was, he wasn't letting it show.

"Seven o'clock this evening," Del said evenly.

Diego had promised himself he would not bring up the subject of Blue unless Del brought it up first. They had met many times since the trial in Miami. He had never once mentioned her name.

Yet Diego knew his meeting with his daughter had had a profound effect on him. He was still going through with his decision to enter a private, little-known program the government had long ago created to help agents such as Seve Delgado start over in a new life when necessary. It was much like the Witness Protection Program, the major difference being the degree to which the person entering the program changed himself prior to entering it. And that once in place, there was no continued support from the program in the new life. Once out, you were on your own.

Diego knew that those were the only terms under which Del would have done anything like this.

"I realize you do not have to report to me any longer. And that technically your answer to my request goes through channels that no longer involve me." Del sat up straight and leaned over the desk. The energy in the room rose along with the tension.

Diego held his gaze, so much like another's. One he missed almost to the point of desperation. An emotion he'd spent three months unsuccessfully trying to bury.

"But in less than four hours I will begin a life that can no longer have anything to do with yours. I have never asked anything of you that wasn't strictly job related. For me to do so now is most difficult. You owe me nothing. You worked for me. We both did our jobs. However, if you have any respect for me, I'd appreciate your letting me leave knowing I am leaving the team in good hands."

Diego felt the crushing weight of Del's request. As hard for Del to make as it was for Diego to bear. The only thing harder was answering him.

"I have great respect for you," he said. "And I do owe you." He lifted his hand to forestall Del's response. "I know I have only spoken of my life once. But over the last three months I have given my past a great deal of examination. Much of it I can no longer make judgments on. I did what I had to do at the time." He looked into Del's eyes. Blue's eyes. "I do know one thing, though. And that is that you saved my life. You gave me a purpose. A focus. And though it took me years to understand, you also gave me something to be proud of, and therefore find pride in."

"Diego, I—"

Diego stopped him again but needed a deep

breath before continuing. "That is why this is so hard for me." He forced himself to maintain eye contact. Understanding was instant, as he knew it would be.

"Then you are turning me down. Turning down the team." He raked a hand through his now brown hair.

It was the first time Diego could recall seeing Del display frustration. Or any emotion for that matter. "I have no choice."

Del pounded the desk with a tight fist. The move was so unexpected, Diego flinched.

"You are the best person to take over this team and you know it." He gestured to Diego's shoulder. "You realize you can't go back into the field."

Diego nodded. His shoulder had healed, but not well enough for him to throw with precision. But that was only part of it. His foot had been more decimated in the Jeep crash than he had let on, or even known. He could walk without a limp now, but his agility was too limited for the jobs he undertook.

"You are the only one who knows this team and how it functions from the inside out. You know the team players, their strengths, how to use them best."

"So does McShane. Promote him."

"That's a nonanswer and you know it. McShane belongs in the field. It's where he wants to be. And frankly he's too independent to ever be a leader. You'd likely all be dead inside a year under his command."

Diego knew Del hadn't meant his indictment harshly. He simply spoke the truth. They both knew it.

"I can't do the job," he said quietly. "Even if I wanted to."

"Do you? I thought this would be exactly what you would want. If I suspected you'd give anything less than the hundred percent you've always given me, I'd never have recommended you."

He knew Del wouldn't leave it alone until Diego gave him a reason to. "Whether I want to or not is immaterial. I can be compromised now. I can't lead the team knowing I can be made vulnerable."

Del's face took on a harsh edge. "You got yourself into a situation like Rico?" He shook his head. "No, I'm sorry, that I just won't buy. Not you."

Like a noose tightening around his neck, there was simply no escaping it. "I would never continue my association with the team if I felt I could be made vulnerable to them. That is why I am respectfully declining your recommendation. I can't take this job, Del."

Del swore long and colorfully and Diego let the man vent, all the while knowing he wasn't off the hook just yet.

"You say you owe me," Del finally said. "If you truly believe that, then tell me the whole thing. It is the only thing I will ever ask of you. No matter your answer, we're square from that point on."

Diego held the older man's dark gaze, seeing his boss, mentor, and father figure in the face before him. He'd give the man what he deserved, what he'd earned. The truth.

"I'm in love with a woman." Even as he spoke the

words Diego knew he'd turned a corner in his life. He was proud of his career and what he'd done for himself and for his country. But it was time to satisfy his own needs. He would no longer be able to conduct his life in shadows and half-truths. He needed to share his secrets, his feelings, his wants, desires, and most important his truths, at his own will, his own discretion. "Your daughter, Blue."

He had no idea what reaction he'd expected, but it was not the obvious relief on Del's face.

"Three months and you never said a word."

Diego didn't have to tell Del that he'd spent most of that time in physical therapy. Then there'd been the fallout of Rico's dismissal from the team and the subsequent altering of the various missions currently under way.

"You haven't mentioned her either," Diego countered.

"I didn't want to influence you. Either of you."

"What is that supposed to mean?"

"It means I have spoken to my daughter a number of times since the trial, and while I don't claim to know everything about the woman she's become, I can tell she is troubled by something."

Diego waited for Del to continue. He had too many questions, several of which he wasn't sure he wanted to hear the answers to anyway.

"I presume you know she sold the cantina to my brother and is going through the academy for the Taos County PD.

Diego nodded. Del apparently understood him as well.

"I know that is what she has wanted. She fits there. In fact, she is second in her class."

If Diego hadn't felt like his whole world was unraveling like a ball of string he'd somehow managed to drop, he'd have smiled at the obvious pride in Del's voice. He did feel vindicated, thought, in his belief that the Delgado family should be reunited.

"She should have done it a long time ago, though I understand why she didn't." Del stood and came around his desk, perching on the edge.

"I am the last person to preach to anyone about the choices one makes in life. I did what I thought was best for Blue and her mother. I have had many regrets for that choice, but I have made peace with my decisions, both good and bad. I have done my best to reconcile that with Blue." He looked away for a moment, then back at Diego. "She is an incredible woman. I wish I could take more credit for that. Her understanding in all of this has been unbelievable, and certainly more than I deserve." He paused to clear his throat.

Diego was riveted to his seat, his own throat growing tight. "Sir, I—"

"No, let me finish. I'm not sure I can do this again."

Diego nodded.

"You completed your job without compromising the mission or your integrity. I know from Blue how badly you wanted to tell her the story. I have never properly thanked you for setting aside your own principles in order to carry out mine." A ghost of a smile curved his lips. "She took great pride in defending your integrity."

Honestly surprised, Diego knew his reaction was obvious.

Del's chuckle defused some of the emotional tension filling the room. "She told me in no uncertain terms that I had demanded more from my team than I had a right to, that I had been a selfish SOB who didn't have enough faith in his own men to allow them to conduct their business as they saw fit."

Diego had no trouble whatsoever picturing her standing up to her father. Something few if any men had ever done. Hell, he'd stalled for months to avoid that very thing himself.

Del grew more serious. "I have known for some time that my daughter has very strong feelings for you. I also knew that you returned those feelings. I recommended you as my replacement knowing this."

"Why?" The question was out before he could stop it.

"Because you needed to make a decision. And to make that decision, you had to have a choice. I still believe you are the right man for the job. I also knew that if you chose to take it, my questions about your feelings for Blue would be answered."

"And now that I've declined?"

"It answers those same questions." He stood and held out his hand. They shook once, then dropped hands.

"It takes a very strong man to understand and respect himself well enough to make the decision you've made." A smile crossed his face. "And if you think you are going to have it easier this way, you are mistaken."

"Sir, you're jumping to conclusions. I'm sorry to have misled you, but I have no intentions of pursuing a relationship with Blue."

Del showed no surprise. "As I said, you're a strong man with strong convictions. Blue thinks she is being fair to you by letting you decide what you want without interference. I say you can't make a fair choice unless you know what all your options are. You have always made the right choices for yourself. I doubt you'll be foolish enough to stop now."

"But, sir—"

"I am flying to Taos to see Blue before I head on to my next destination."

Diego didn't ask for any details about Del's future, knowing there would be no answers.

"There is room on the plane for you." He didn't wait for a reply, just strode to the door. He turned back before leaving. "Gate C-two." Then he was gone.

TWELVE

Blue sited down the target, then squeezed the trigger. The small pile of rocks flew into the air. When the echo died, the air was perfectly still, yet something shifted. Awareness made the hair on her neck prickle as she turned.

Diego Santerra stood ten yards away. The sun silhouetted his rugged frame against the backdrop of Red Rock Mesa.

"I didn't hear you approach."

"You were concentrating pretty fiercely on your targets."

So he'd been standing there for more than a few seconds. She looked past him but saw no bike or other transportation. "How did you get up here?"

"My Jeep is at the bottom. I hiked up."

He was wearing jeans, hiking boots, and a short-sleeve T-shirt. There was no knife strapped to his wrist, but he wore a clip on his waistband. The same man, and yet not the same at all. She saw no evidence of his injuries. But she'd badgered her father into telling her just how severe they had been, and she knew the hike up the rocky terrain had been far from easy. She also knew about her father's recommendation and why he'd made it.

She was to meet her father in several hours. She had no idea what to make of Diego's return. She didn't dare let herself hope.

"Why are you here?"

With the sun in her eyes, she wasn't sure, but she could have sworn he almost smiled. "Do they let you bully people at the academy?"

"No," she responded, as helpless against his quiet charm now as she had been three months ago. "That's why I have to take it out on everyone else." She slipped the rifle sling over her head and laid the gun down on the case by her feet. "Why did you come back, Diego?"

If he noticed the slight tremor in her voice, or the way she'd locked her knees to keep them from shaking, he wasn't obvious about it.

"About five years ago I rescued a South American priest from some Bolivian terrorists. I had to kill several of them to get him out. Even though they'd beaten him severely and starved him half to death, he was very torn over the fact that I'd taken lives in order to save his."

Blue remained silent, her anxiety forgotten.

"He didn't thank me. Instead he asked me if I was remorseful, if I felt I'd sinned. I told him I was just doing my job. He prayed for me, just as he prayed for the men who had kidnapped and beaten him. I asked him if it was better to let a good man like himself be killed in order to keep from killing men like his kidnappers. He said it was not his job to decide who was good or bad, that there was good and bad in all men. I asked him what he would have done. He thought about it for a long time, then finally said that his choice should have been to try to find another path in order to gain his freedom. That there was a better way for the terrorists to achieve their goals too."

"He said he *should* have chosen that," Blue said. "Did he tell you what he truly would have done?"

Diego nodded. "He said that his first reaction when I asked him was that he would have killed them. It was that reaction, the anger he had for them that he hadn't been able to reconcile. Though he hadn't killed them, he felt as if he'd committed the sin anyway. I told him that his faith didn't preclude him from being human, from being a man."

"What did he say?"

"He looked at me and said that maybe the real sin was in not being honest with yourself. In pretending to be what you think you should be instead of confronting what you truly are and coming to peace with that."

"Have you come to peace with who you are?" she asked.

"I thought I had."

"And now?"

"I'm not so sure. I turned your father down."

Honestly surprised, Blue asked, "And you regret that now? It's not too late—"

"That's what I'm hoping. He walked to her, stopping less than a foot away. "I have always been honest with myself about who I am and the life I've led. I was honest with your father about why I couldn't lead the team."

"But you want to anyway?"

"No. That decision stands. I've had a hard time being honest with myself about what I really want. I told myself that I was doing the right thing in not reaching for what I wanted, even though it felt wrong. Your father made me realize that what I thought was nobility and selflessness was really cowardice and fear. Fear of trying and failing. Fear of wanting something so badly and not getting it. That is why I'm here."

"To come to peace with it or to go after what you want?"

"In order to do the first, I have to do the second."

Blue swallowed the knot in her throat. "And what is it you want?"

He took another step, casting a shadow between them that allowed her into his pale blue eyes.

"You. I want you. I love you, Blue."

Blue almost put her hand to her chest to keep her heart from bursting through her skin. She wanted to throw herself into his arms, but held back. He deserved the same honesty he'd shown her.

"I told myself that I was doing what I wanted, enrolling in the academy, and that you needed to choose for yourself what you wanted. That's why I didn't contact you.

"Maybe the real sin here is in making a choice without allowing the other person involved to have a say," she continued. "You are right. It's easy to mistake nobility for fear. I thought that by becoming a police officer, I was conquering my fear. But you know what?"

"What?"

The raw emotion in that one word pulled Blue a step closer to Diego. "When I came back from Florida, I had no doubts about selling the cantina and enrolling. I knew it was right. You gave me the strength to see that. But there is something else I want even more. And I was terrified to try and fail, so I told myself I was doing the right thing to avoid facing it."

"What do you want, Blue?"

She closed the distance between them and laid her hand against his cheek. They both trembled.

"I want you, Diego Santerra."

He pulled her into his arms, weaving a hand through her hair. "No more fear," he whispered.

"No more facing choices alone."

He kissed her and she returned it, taking and giving soft kisses, exploring slowly, gently, until Diego finally lifted his mouth away from hers.

"We'll face what we want together and make it work, Blue."

"Does that mean no more sinning?"

Diego's smile was slow and sexy. "Well, I had thought about making an honest woman out of you."

"You already have." She kissed him. "I love you. I want you." She kissed him again. "And now that I have you, I intend to keep you. How's that for honesty?"

He looped his arms around her waist and pulled her to him. "I think I sort of like the idea of being a kept man, but actually I thought I'd get a job too."

Blue marveled at how naturally their bodies fit together, how right he felt. She rested her arms on his shoulders, playing with the ends of his hair.

"What do you want to do?" she asked, knowing his answer would not alter how she felt. She'd support him in his choice just as he had hers.

"Your father put me in touch with a newly formed agency based in Colorado, just outside of Denver. Basically they set up defensive-tactics training schools. It's mostly geared to government agencies, both well known and not so well known. But they are already looking to link the schools to other countries and combine forces with their trainers."

His enthusiasm was so genuine, she had to laugh. "Sounds perfect."

"There's only one problem. I'd have to go before you completed academy training."

"Well, I've already talked to Gerraro about the Taos PD. Actually he talked to me. He seems to think that I'd find more of what I want, law-enforcement-wise, in a bigger city. And if I want to make detective down the line, I think he is right."

"Denver is a city."

She grinned. "My thoughts exactly."

"Marry me, Blue."

"Yes," she said instantly, then kissed him. "On one condition," she added.

"Name it."

"Take me skiing for our honeymoon?" Blue was surprised when Diego suddenly looked uncomfortable.

Understanding dawned. "Your foot. You can't ski." She kissed him then caressed his cheek, a hot thrill stealing through her when his eyes lit yet again at her casual touch. "It's okay, really. I was kidding."

"It's not my foot. But you're right, I can't ski." He actually looked sheepish. "At least I don't know if I can."

"I'll stay with you on the bunny slopes as long as necessary," she said with mock sympathy.

"We'll see who outslaloms who," he shot back.

"We really must work on your confidence."

He pulled her head to his and kissed her long and hard. "This is only the beginning, Blue. I promise you I'll work as hard at being your husband as I've ever done anything else. I love you."

"And I love you. I promise you'll never be rid of me."

"I'll hold you to that."

She squeezed him tighter. "I was counting on it. I'll let you ride my Harley down the mountain if you teach me how to throw that knife you're wearing."

"Do I sense a bargaining pattern developing here?"

She smiled and whispered in his ear.

He grinned, then scooped her up in his arms.

Blue let out a yelp. "I didn't mean right now, right here. Put me down before you strain something."

"The key to bargaining is compromise," he said, walking over to the Harley. "The knife throwing can wait, but I'll let you make the choice." Then he whispered in her ear.

"Why, yes," she said with a wicked grin. "Choice is a very good thing indeed."

THE EDITORS' CORNER

Begin your holiday celebration early with the four new LOVESWEPT romances coming your way next month. Packed with white-hot emotion, each of these novels is the best getaway from the hustle and bustle typical of this time of year. So set aside a few hours for yourself, cuddle up with the books, and enjoy!

THE DAMARON MARK: THE LION, LOVESWEPT #814, is the next enticing tale in Fayrene Preston's bestselling Damaron Mark series. Lion Damaron is too gorgeous to be real, a walking heartbreaker leaning against a wrecked sports car, when Gabi St. Armand comes to his rescue! She doesn't dare let his seductive smile persuade her he is serious, but flirting with the wealthy hunk is reckless fun—and the only way she can disguise the desire that scorches her very soul. Fayrene Preston beguiles once more with her irresistible tale of unexpected, impossible love that simply must be.

TALL, DARK, AND BAD is the perfect description for the hero in Charlotte Hughes's newest LOVESWEPT, #815. He storms her grandmother's dinner party like a warrior claiming his prize, but when Cooper Garrett presses Summer Pettigrew against the nearest wall and captures her mouth, she has no choice but to surrender. He agrees to play her fiancé in a breathless charade, but no game of let's pretend can be this steamy, this erotic. Get set for a story that's both wickedly funny and wildly arousing, as only Charlotte Hughes can tell it.

For her holiday offering, Peggy Webb helps Santa decide who's **NAUGHTY AND NICE**, #816. Benjamin Sullivan III knows trouble when he spots it in a redhead's passionate glare, but figuring out why Holly Jones is plotting against the town's newest arrival is a mystery too fascinating to ignore! How can she hunger so for a handsome scoundrel? Holly wonders, even as she finds herself charmed, courted, and carried away by Ben's daredevil grin. Award-winning author Peggy Webb makes mischief utterly sexy and wins hearts with teasing tenderness!

Suzanne Brockmann's seductive and inventive romance tangles readers in **THE KISSING GAME**, LOVESWEPT, #817. Allowing Simon Hunt to play her partner on her latest assignment probably isn't Frankie Paresky's best idea ever, but the P.I. finds it just as hard as most women do to tell him no! When a chase to solve a long-ago mystery sparks a sizzling attraction between old friends, Frankie wavers between pleasure and panic. Simon's the best bad boy she's ever known, and he just might turn out to be the man she'll always love. Suzanne Brockmann delivers pure pleasure from the first page to the last.

Happy reading!

With warmest wishes,

Beth de Guzman   Shauna Summers

Senior Editor   Editor

P.S. Watch for these Bantam women's fiction titles coming in December: Join *New York Times* bestselling author Sandra Brown for **BREAKFAST IN BED**, available in mass-market. Kay Hooper, nationally bestselling author of *AMANDA*, weaves a tale of mystery when two strangers are drawn together by one fatal moment in **AFTER CAROLINE.** The long-out-of-print classic **LOVE'S A STAGE,** by the beloved writing team Sharon and Tom Curtis, is back for your pleasure. And for her Bantam Books debut, Patricia Coughlin presents **LORD SAVAGE.** Don't miss the previews of these exceptional novels in next month's LOVESWEPTs.

If you're into the world of computers and would like current information on Bantam's women's fiction, visit our Web site, ISN'T IT ROMANTIC, at the following address: **http://www.bdd.com/romance.**

And immediately following this page, sneak a peek at the Bantam women's fiction titles on sale *now*!

She was a slave to his passion . . . but he was the master of her heart

SHADOWS AND LACE

a stunning novel of captive love
by national bestseller

Teresa Medeiros

With one roll of the dice, the shameful deed was done. Baron Lindsey Fordyce had gambled and lost, and now his beautiful daughter, Rowena, was about to pay the price. Spirited away to an imposing castle, the fiery innocent found herself pressed into the service of a dark and forbidding knight accused of murder . . . and much more. Handsome, brooding Sir Gareth of Caerleon had spent years waiting for this chance for revenge. But when he sought to use the fair Rowena to slay the ghosts of his tortured past, he never imagined he'd be ensnared in a silken trap of his own making—slave to a desire he could never hope to quench. . . .

Rowena came bursting in like a ray of sunshine cutting through the stale layer of smoke that hung over the hall. The wild, sweet scent of the moor clung to her hair, her skin, the handwoven tunic she wore. Her cheeks were touched with the flushed rose of exertion; her eyes were alight with exuberance.

She ran straight to her father, her words tumbling out faster than the apples dumped from the sack she clutched upside down.

"Oh, Papa, I am ever so happy you've come home! Where did you have the stallion hidden? He is the most beautiful animal I ever saw. Did you truly find your elusive fortune this journey?"

Falling to her knees beside his chair, she pulled a crumpled bunch of heather from her pocket and dumped it in his lap without giving him time to reply.

"I brought your favorite flowers and Little Freddie has promised to cook apples on the coals. They will be hot and sweet and juicy, just as you like them. 'Twill be a hundred times better than any nasty old roasted hare. Oh, Papa, you're home! We thought you were never coming back."

She threw her arms around his waist. The uninhibited gesture knocked the cap from her head to unleash a cascade of wheaten curls.

Fordyce's arms did not move to encircle her. He sat stiff in her embrace. She lifted her face, aware of a silence broken only by the thump of a log shifting on the fire. Her father did not meet her eyes, and for one disturbing moment, she thought she saw his lower lip tremble.

She followed his gaze. Her brothers stood lined up before the hearth in the most ordered manner she had ever seen them. Irwin beamed from the middle of the row.

Bathed in the light of the flickering fire, the stranger stepped out of the shadows. Rowena raised her eyes. From where she knelt, it was as if she was peering up from the bottom of a deep well to meet the eyes of the man who towered over her. His level gaze sent a bolt of raw fear through her, riveting her to the floor as she stared into the face of death itself. A long moment passed before she could pull her eyes away.

"Papa?" she breathed, patting his cool, trembling hand.

He stroked her hair, his eyes distant. "Rowena, I believe 'twould be fitting for you to step outside till we have concluded our dealings."

"You made no mention of a daughter, Fordyce." The stranger's gaze traveled between father and child.

Papa's arm curved around Rowena's shoulders like a shield. The stranger's mocking laughter echoed through the hall. Only Rowena heard Papa's muttered curse as he realized what he had done.

"Your interest is in my sons," Papa hissed, a tiny vein in his temple beginning to throb.

"But *your* interest is not. That much is apparent."

The man advanced and Rowena rose, knowing instinctively that she did not want to be on her knees at this stranger's feet. She stood without flinching to face the wrought links of the silver chain mail that crossed the man's chest. From broad shoulders to booted feet, his garments were as black as the eyes that regarded her with frank scrutiny. She returned his perusal with arms crossed in front of her.

A closer look revealed his eyes were not black, but a deep, velvety brown. Their opacity rendered them inscrutable, but alive with intelligence. Heavy, arched brows added a mocking humor that gave Rowena the impression she was being laughed at, although his expression did not waver. His sable hair was neatly cut, but an errant waviness warned of easy rebellion. His well-formed features were saved from prettiness by an edge of rugged masculinity enhanced by his sheer size. The thought flitted through Rowena's mind that he might be handsome if his face was not set in such ruthless lines.

He reached down and lifted a strand of her hair as if hypnotized at its brightness. The velvety tendril curled around his fingers at the caress.

Rowena's hand slipped underneath her tunic, but before she could bring the knife up to strike, her wrist was twisted in a fearful grip that sent the blade clattering to the stones. She bit her lip to keep from crying out. The man loosed her.

"She has more fire than the rest of you combined." The stranger strode back to the hearth. "I'll take her."

The hall exploded in enraged protest. Papa sank back in the chair, his hand over his eyes.

"You cannot have my sister!" Little Freddie's childish tenor cut through his brothers' cries.

The man leaned against the hearth with a smirk. "Take heart, lad. 'Tis not forever. She is only to serve me for a year."

Rowena looked at Papa. His lips moved with no sound. Her brothers spewed forth dire and violent threats, although they remained in place as if rooted to the stone. She wondered if they had all taken leave of their senses. The stranger's sparkling eyes offered no comfort. They watched her as if delighting in the chaos he had provoked. The tiny lines around them crinkled as he gave her a wink made all the more threatening by its implied intimacy. A primitive thrill of fear shot through her, freezing her questions before they could leave her lips.

Papa's whine carried just far enough to reach the man's ears. "We said sons, did we not?"

The man's booming voice silenced them all. "Nay, Fordyce. We said children. I was to have the use of one of your children for a year."

Rowena's knees went as slack as her jaw. Only the sheer effort of her will kept her standing.

"You cannot take a man's only daughter," said Papa, unable to keep the pleading note from his voice. "Show me some mercy, won't you?"

The knight snorted. "Mercy? What have you ever known of mercy, Fordyce? I've come to teach you of justice."

Papa mustered his courage and banged with force on the arm of the chair. "I will not allow it."

The stranger's hand went to the hilt of the massive sword sheathed at his waist. Beneath the rich linen of his surcoat, the muscles in his arms rippled with the slight gesture. "You choose to fight?" he asked softly.

Lindsey Fordyce hesitated the merest moment. "Rowena, you must accompany this nice man."

Rowena blinked stupidly, thrown off guard by her father's abrupt surrender.

Little Freddie charged forward, an iron pot wielded over his head like a bludgeon. The knight turned with sword drawn. Rowena lunged for his arm, but Papa sailed past both of them and knocked the boy to the ground with a brutal uppercut. Freddie glared at his father, blood trickling from his mouth and nose.

"Don't be an idiot," Papa spat. "He will only kill you, and then he will kill me."

Still wielding his sword, the stranger faced the row of grumbling boys. "If anyone cares to challenge my right to their sister, I shall be more than happy to defend it."

The broad blade gleamed in the firelight. Big Freddie returned the man's stare for a long moment, his callused paws clenched into fists. He turned away and rested his forehead against the warm stones of the hearth.

The stranger's eyes widened as Irwin's plump form stepped forward, trumpet still clutched in hand. Papa took one step toward Irwin, who then plopped his ample bottom on the hearth and studied the trumpet as if seeing it for the first time.

"A wager is a wager." Papa ran his thumbs along the worn gilt of his tattered surcoat. "As you well know, I am a baron and a knight myself—an honorable man."

He sighed as if the burden of his honor was too much for him to bear. The short laugh uttered by the knight was not a pleasant sound.

Papa gently took Rowena's face between his moist palms. "Go with him, Rowena." He swallowed with difficulty. "He will not harm you."

The stranger watched the exchange in cryptic silence, his arms crossed over his chest.

Rowena searched her father's face, blindly hoping for a burst of laughter to explain away the knight's intrusion as a cruel jest. The hope that flickered within her sputtered and died, smothered by the bleakness in the cornflower-blue eyes that were a pale, rheumy echo of her own.

"I shall go with him, Papa, if you say I should."

The man moved forward, unlooping the rope at his waist. Papa stepped back to keep a healthy sword's distance away from the imposing figure.

Rowena shoved her hands behind her back. "There is no need to bind me."

The man retrieved her hands. Rowena did not

flinch as he bound her wrists in front of her none too gently.

Her soft tone belied her anger. "If Papa says I am to go with you, then I will go."

The dark head remained bowed as he tightened the knot with a stiff jerk. Coiling the free end of the rope around his wrist, he led her to the door without a word. She slowed to scoop up her cap. Feeling the sudden tautness in the rope, the man tugged. Rowena dug her heels into the flagstones, resisting his pull. Their eyes met in a silent battle of wills. Without warning, he yanked the rope, causing Rowena to stumble. She straightened, her eyes shining with angry tears for an instant. Then their blue depths cleared and she purposefully followed him through the door, cap clutched in bound hands.

The boys shuffled after them like the undead in a grim processional. Papa meandered behind. Little Freddie was gripped between two of his brothers; a fierce scowl darkened his fair brow.

Night had fallen. A full moon cast its beams through the scant trees, suffusing the muted landscape with the eerie glow of a bogus daylight. Big Freddie gave a low, admiring whistle as a white stallion seemed to rise from the thin shroud of mist that cloaked the ground. The fog entwined itself around the graceful fetlocks. The creature pranced nervously at the sound of approaching footsteps.

Rowena's eyes were drawn to the golden bridle crowning the massive animal. Jewels of every hue encrusted its length. Why would a man of such wealth come all the way to Revelwood to steal a poor man's child? The knight's forbidding shoulders invited no questions as he mounted the horse and slipped Rowena's tether over the leather pommel. The horse's iron-shod hooves twitched. How close could she follow without being pounded to a pulp?

Irwin stepped in front of the horse as if accustomed to placing his bulk in the path of a steed mounted by a fully armed nobleman. The knight leaned back in the saddle with a sigh.

"Kind sir?" Irwin's voice was a mere squeak, so he cleared his throat and tried again. "Kind sir, I hasten to remind you that you are stealing away our only ray of light in a life of darkness. You pluck the single bloom in our garden of grim desolation. I speak for all of us."

Irwin's cousins looked at one another and scratched their heads. Rowena wished faintly that the knight would run him through and end her embarrassment.

"You make an eloquent plea, lad," the knight replied, surprising them all. "Mayhaps you should plead with her father to make his wagers with more care in the future."

From behind Big Freddie, Papa dared to shoot the man a look of pure hatred.

"You will not relent?" asked Irwin.

"I will not."

"Then I pray the burden of chivalry rests heavily on your shoulders. I pray you will honor my sweet cousin with the same consideration you would grant to the rest of the fair and weaker sex."

Rowena itched to box his ears, remembering the uncountable times she had wrestled him to the ground and pinched him until he squealed for mercy.

The stranger again uttered that short, unpleasant laugh. "Do not fear, lad. I will grant her the same consideration that I would grant to any wench as comely as she. Now stand aside or be trampled."

Irwin tripped to the left as the knight kicked the stallion into a trot. Rowena broke into a lope to avoid being jerked off her feet. She dared break her concentration only long enough for one last hungry look at her family. She heard the soft thud of fist pummeling flesh and a familiar cry as Little Freddie tackled Irwin in blind rage and frustration.

Then they were gone. She focused all of her attention on the rocky turf beneath her feet as her world narrowed to the task of putting one foot in front of the other without falling nose first into the drumming hooves.

THE MARRIAGE WAGER

by

Jane Ashford

After watching her husband gamble his life away, Lady Emma Tarrant was determined to prevent another young man from meeting a similar fate. So she challenged the scoundrel who held his debts to another game. After eight years of war, Colin Wareham thought he'd seen it all, but when Lady Emma accosted him, he was suddenly intrigued—and aroused. So he named his stakes: a loss, and he'd forgive the debts. A win, and the lady must give him her heart. . . .

"Will you discard, sir?"

He looked as if he wished to speak, but in the end he simply laid down a card. Focusing on her hand, Emma tried to concentrate all her attention upon it. But she was aware now of his gaze upon her, of his compelling presence on the other side of the table.

She looked up again. He *was* gazing at her, steadily, curiously. But she could find no threat in his eyes. On the contrary, they were disarmingly friendly. He could not possibly look like that and wish her any harm, Emma thought dreamily.

He smiled.

Emma caught her breath. His smile was amazing—warm, confiding, utterly trustworthy. She must have misjudged him, Emma thought.

"Are you sure you won't have some of this excellent brandy?" he asked, sipping from his glass. "I really can recommend it."

Seven years of hard lessons came crashing back upon Emma as their locked gaze broke. He was doing this on purpose, of course. Trying to divert her attention, beguile her into making mistakes and losing. Gathering all her bitterness and resolution, Emma shifted her mind to the cards. She would not be caught so again.

Emma won the second hand, putting them even. But as she exulted in the win, she noticed a small smile playing around Colin Wareham's lips and wondered at it. He poured himself another glass of brandy and sipped it. He looked as if he was thoroughly enjoying himself, she thought. And he didn't seem at all worried that she might beat him. His arrogance was infuriating.

All now rested on the third hand. As she opened a new pack of cards and prepared to deal, Emma took a deep breath.

"You are making a mistake, refusing this brandy," Colin said, sipping again.

"I have no intention of fuzzing my wits with drink," answered Emma crisply. She did not look at him as she snapped out the cards.

"Who are you?" he said abruptly. "Where do you come from? You have the voice and manner of a nobleman's daughter, but you are nothing like the women I meet in society."

Emma flushed a little. There was something in his tone—it might be admiration or derision—that made her self-conscious. Let some of those women spend the last seven years as she had, she thought bitterly, and then see what they were like. "I came here to play cards," she said coldly. "I have said I do not wish to converse with you."

Raising one dark eyebrow, he picked up his hand. The fire hissed in the grate. One of the candles guttered, filling the room with the smell of wax and smoke. At this late hour, the streets outside were silent; the only sounds were Ferik's surprisingly delicate snores from the hall.

In silence, they frowned over discards and calculated odds. Finally, after a long struggle, Wareham said, "I believe this point is good." He put down a card.

Emma stared at it.

"And also my quint," he added, laying down another.

Emma's eyes flickered to his face, then down again.

"Yes?" he urged.

Swallowing, she nodded.

"Ah. Good. Then—a quint, a tierce, fourteen aces, three kings, and eleven cards played, ma'am."

Emma gazed at the galaxy of court cards which he spread before her, then fixed on the one card he still held. The game depended on it, and there was no hint to tell her what she should keep to win the day. She hesitated a moment longer, then made her decision. "A diamond," she said, throwing down the rest of her hand.

"Too bad," he replied, exhibiting a small club.

Emma stared at the square of pasteboard, stunned. She couldn't believe that he had beaten her. "Piqued, repiqued, and capotted," she murmured. It was a humiliating defeat for one with her skill.

"Bad luck."

"I cannot believe you kept that club."

"Rather than throw it away on the slender chance of picking up an ace or a king?"

Numbly, Emma nodded. "You had been taking such risks."

"I sometimes bet on the slim chances," he conceded. "But you must vary your play if you expect to keep your opponent off-balance." He smiled.

That charming smile, Emma thought. Not gloating or contemptuous, but warm all the way to those extraordinary eyes. It almost softened the blow of losing. Almost.

"We said nothing of your stake for this game," he pointed out.

"You asked me for none," Emma retorted. She could not nearly match the amount of Robin Bellingham's notes.

"True." He watched as she bit her lower lip in frustration, and savored the rapid rise and fall of her breasts under the thin bodice of her satin gown. "It appears we are even."

She pounded her fist softly on the table. She had been sure she could beat him, Colin thought. And she had not planned beyond that point. He waited, curious to see what she would do now.

She pounded the table again, thwarted determination obvious in her face. "Will you try another match?" she said finally.

A fighter, Colin thought approvingly. He breathed in the scent of her perfume, let his eyes linger on the creamy skin of her shoulders. He had never encountered such a woman before. He didn't want her to go. On the contrary, he found himself wanting something quite different. "One hand," he offered. "If you win, the notes are yours."

"And if I do not?" she asked.

"You may still have them, but I get . . ." He hesitated. He was not the sort of man who seduced young ladies for sport. But she had come here to his house and challenged him, Colin thought. She was no schoolgirl. She had intrigued and irritated and roused him.

"What?" she said rather loudly.

He had been staring at her far too intensely, Colin realized. But the brandy and the strangeness of the night had made him reckless. "You," he replied.